Hearts in Trim

by Lavinia R. Davis

Hearts
in Trim

Doubleday & Company, Inc., Garden City, New York

For
Frances Riker Davis
alias Benzedrine

Contents

Hearts in Trim

I

Squeak On Christmas Eve the Bruce family finished supper early and by eight-thirty each member of the family was filling in the time before the late carol service in his or her particular way. Johnny, 8, licked the bowl while Mrs. Hilsen, the part-time cook, iced a Norwegian Christmas cake. Mrs. Bruce wrote a letter at her desk in the library and Mr. Bruce read *Walden* sitting in the Morris chair between the fireplace and the Christmas tree. The two elder girls, Alice, who was home from her sophomore year at Smith, and Sunny, who was going to be married to Charlie Reed in January, were up in their double room sorting out clothes.

Only Serena, usually known as Squeak, the youngest daughter in the family, had not settled down to anything definite. Way back last summer she had made elaborate plans to decorate the stone lions on old Mrs. Frostgate's place on Christmas Eve, but she hadn't thought of that since September. Right now she decided to wrap up the toy pistol holster she had bought at the last minute for Johnny, but when she looked for her Christmas paper she couldn't find it. "Have you seen my wrapping paper, Mum? I'm sure I left it here in the library."

Mrs. Bruce shook her head, handed Squeak some of her own paper, and then before she went back to her letter picked up a message Mrs. Hilsen had left on her desk. "Oh, by the way, Cliff

Hawks telephoned. Apparently he's staying with his grandmother over the holidays."

Squeak groaned. Cliff's mother was dead and his father had remarried twice and for years Cliff had drifted in and out of Stapleton on short, irregular visits to his grandmother Hawks. Even at Johnny's age Squeak had understood why Mum and Dad were sorry for Cliff, but that hadn't helped a bit when he had broken up her carefully planned ninth birthday party by putting a rubber mouse in the lemonade. "Do I have to call him back?" she said out loud. "Do I have to?"

"Oh no. I don't think so," Mum said. "He'll call back if it's important and besides it says here he wanted to speak to any one of you girls."

Squeak said nothing, but the faint sympathy she had felt for Cliff vanished. If he wanted to speak to Sunny or Alice, why didn't he say so? She began rummaging behind the Canterbury for her paper and had just thought of telephoning Lyb Harris, who was her best friend at high school, when Mum spoke. "What are you going to do now, darling? Help Mrs. Hilsen clean up?"

"Oh, I think Mrs. Hilsen's practically finished," Squeak said, and, suddenly inspired, went on more quickly. "I thought perhaps I'd walk up to the church and meet you all there. I haven't really seen the Christmas lights and the village ought to be beautiful now it's snowing."

"I don't know about doing that alone," Mrs. Bruce began, and even as she spoke the idea grew brighter and more enticing in Squeak's mind. It wasn't just a lonely walk through the snow. It was more of a pilgrimage, a Christmas pilgrimage!

"Please, please let me," she said, and Mrs. Bruce shrugged resignedly.

"Well, all right, but be sure to wrap up warmly and to start in plenty of time. You ought to leave here not later than nine-thirty if you are going to walk."

Squeak was too enamored by her growing dream to do more than nod before she started up to her own room. As she passed the girls' room she thought of her wrapping paper again and stopped in to see if either of them had taken it. They hadn't, but as she glanced over the table by the dormer window she saw a book of poetry by John Donne which she hadn't seen before and began to turn the pages. The line "All love is wonder" caught her attention and she read the rest of the stanza and then turned to Alice. "Where did this come from, Al? Are you reading it at college?"

"English A," Alice said. "But it's not for the likes of you, honey chile. John Donne's really tough going."

Squeak bridled. "What do you think I am, Johnny's age and just graduating to A. A. Milne?"

"Of course not!" Sunny looked up from the floor, where she was sorting stockings. "Alice knows you're a marvelous reader. What is the book, anyway? A novel?"

"Poetry. And definitely difficult," Alice said, and then, seeing that Squeak still held the book, waved good-naturedly. "Help yourself, chum. But if you don't like it don't say I didn't warn you."

Squeak took the book and went on to her own room, but it was so cluttered that there was no room to sit down. For a while the decoration of the room had reflected by turns each of Squeak's most pressing interests. Horses. Movie stars. A craze for interior decorating. Then the year she was confirmed, a nun's cell, or at least her own idea of one. After that when Alice went to Smith it blossomed with collegiate banners. Right now it was a jumble of all these phases, while books, which were Squeak's most constant interest, crowded the bookshelves, the desk, the radiator, and the one comfortable chair where of all things the Christmas paper lay beside her scarf and pocketbook.

She thought for a moment of starting the tidying bee Mrs. Hilsen had been suggesting for weeks, decided it would take too long, and flopped down on the bed with the book in her hand.

Five minutes later she realized that perhaps lying down was a mistake. Her bed was wonderfully comfortable and her room was cozily warm for the first time all day. Also John Donne was much duller than she had expected. Not too difficult, of course—Alice was wrong about that—but definitely dull and unexpectedly full of death and worms and corruption. The line "All love is wonder" was beautiful, but you had to plow through so much to find others like it. For the most part Donne's idea of love seemed both coarse and tormented. Not a bit like "The Idyll," she thought, and yawned as she skipped to another page.

"The Idyll" was Squeak's own and strictly secret invention. It was a long unwritten story, which she had thought about so often that it had a name, a shimmering personality of its own, which separated it from more fleeting and less important daydreams. No, Donne was definitely not like "The Idyll," which was always about the same tall, dark, beautifully sophisticated hero and herself.

She turned past the poems to the sermons and would have skipped those entirely if an underlined passage had not attracted her attention. "God emploies several translators," she read, and now her eyes were so brimming with sleep she could hardly see. The book slipped a little in her hands, but she gripped it more firmly, determined to tell Alice how much of it she had read. She tried a few more lines, but her eyes stung so that she simply had to close them. The book slipped again and landed gently on top of her stomach. She sighed, but before she could pull herself together enough to move the book she was asleep.

In the meantime the snow outside fell more slowly and then stopped. It had not been a heavy fall, but there was enough to cover the Bruces' fields, shroud the barberry bushes, and soften the outlines of the little old building that had once, long before the Bruces had owned the place, been a cobbler's shed. The narrow black-top road that led past the Bruces' house up to the village of Stapleton was a trackless path of white and the village itself was transformed from a humdrum workaday commuting town to a New England Bethlehem.

Even the forbidding Victorian houses on Moose Ridge looked gracious and welcoming with snow-covered lawns and Christmas lights at the doorways. There were no lights at the old Frostgate place, but the stone lions which guarded the driveway looked unusually fine with snowy blankets and snowy whiskers. In fact when the moon came out and turned the whole world silvery the lions were magnificent, which was a waste in a way because there was nobody there to see them. Old Mrs. Frostgate had been dead and buried for five months. The cousin who had inherited the place was dining at the Village Inn and Squeak Bruce, who loved the lions, was very sound asleep indeed.

By that time, in the big double room down the hall from where Squeak slept, Alice had finished going through her bureau drawers and was giving herself a manicure, but Sunny, who had been christened Sarah, was still looking over her stockings.

"You've gone over that same pile three times," Alice said, and blew on her nails to dry the polish. "I swear, I think you're worse about making up your mind than Squeak."

Sunny smiled and the way her face lit up more than justified her nickname. "Well, you see, I know these are usable, but with all the trousseau ones I really don't *need* them and I was wondering if Mrs. Hilsen would be offended if I gave them to her."

"Don't ask her," Alice said. "Just give 'em to me instead. Ever since the second week of college I've been so bankrupt that if Grandpa doesn't crash through with cash money tomorrow I'm going to sue him for breach of promise."

"Alice!" Sunny's gentle voice was shocked. "What a way to talk about a Christmas present. Really, darling."

Alice grinned, amused at Sunny's characteristic reaction, and secretly secure in the knowledge that she was the only one in the family who had inherited their mother's efficiency about money as well as other practical things. "Well," she said out loud, "can I have the stockings?"

"Of course you can," Sunny said, and long before she had finished straightening out the back of her bottom drawer Alice had matched the stockings, rolled them neatly, and dropped them into her own bureau. "Thanks," she said, and began to brush her short brown hair, which was darker than Sunny's harvest-gold waves, also crisper and curlier and easier to do. "Oughtn't you to be getting ready for church? Mum said we'd be leaving at ten-thirty, and Charlie's sure to call for you earlier."

Sunny still sat on the floor in a happy trance. "Isn't it marvelous the way things work out if you just go on trusting and let them?" she said. "First my not going to college, so I met Charlie right away when his family moved here three years ago, and then our getting engaged last summer, and now his getting Christmas leave as well as ten days in January for our honeymoon. I nearly dropped dead when he called up from camp last night and told me to meet him at the station this morning."

"Better come to life and get ready to meet him again," Alice said dryly. "And don't forget that Jube Carter has Tom Connaught staying with him and you're both expected at the Carters' after the carol service. Tom's counting on seeing Charlie."

Sunny finally stood up and began to change her shoes, but her gentle, rather vague blue eyes were still on Alice. "Do you like Jube?" she asked. "Really like him, I mean?"

Alice laughed. "No," she said. "Definitely not in the way you mean and in every other way definitely yes. Besides it's handy that he and Tom are both going to be ushers for Charlie and it's even handier having Jube at Williams while I'm at Smith."

At that moment the front doorbell rang and they both heard men's voices, the scrape of their mother's desk chair, and her quick, firm footsteps. "Charlie dear, how wonderful to see you. The Air Force agrees with you marvelously. Sunny will be down in a moment. Johnny, run up and tell all three of the girls to hurry. We're leaving Mrs. Hilsen home on the way to church, so we ought to start ourselves."

Johnny pounded up the stairs and burst into the girls' room. "Charlie's here," he panted, "and Mum says we've got to get going and gee he looks swell in that blue uniform, but I wish he had some medals."

He spoke to an inattentive audience because Alice had already started down the hall and Sunny, putting on her hat as she ran, was only a few steps behind. "Charlie. Oh, Charlie," she called out. "I am so sorry I wasn't ready, but you see . . ."

Johnny never heard the rest of Sunny's sentence because just then Mrs. Hilsen came upstairs to make sure he washed his hands and brushed his hair, and a moment later Mother called out: "Johnny. Serena! Do hurry, children. Charles and Sunny have left already and Dad and Alice have gone to get the car."

Johnny turned and ducked under Mrs. Hilsen's arm. "Go ahead," he told her. "I forgot to call Squeak."

She was still sound asleep when he reached her small third-floor bedroom. "Squeak. Wake up," he said, and gave her arm a jerk, so that John Donne thumped to the floor. "We're leaving. For the carol service. Right this ninstant."

Squeak's dark eyes blinked open and she stared at her small brother. "You look nice," she said sleepily, and then she heard the toot of the car horn and Mother's voice floating up the stairs. "Hurry, children. Do hurry. You know how your father hates to be late for church."

Squeak jumped off the bed, scuffled on her loafers, and reached out for her comb. Her brown hair was straighter and finer than the rest of the family's and inclined to be wispy unless she brushed it carefully. It was definitely wispy now, but there was no time to do anything about it when she still had to find her hat, which she wore so seldom it was always lost when she needed it. She compromised by putting on her new, best lipstick, and then dove into her closet to look for her hat. She found it finally, lint-covered and crumpled on the floor, swooped it on, hauled her coat over one shoulder, and started down the stairs.

The rest of the family were all in the car by the time she dashed out of doors. Mother, Johnny, and Mrs. Hilsen were in back. Father, with Alice beside him, was in front. "Serena." "Squeak!" "Squeak." "Serena!" Four voices shouted to her at once, and then Mother's voice, clear and carrying, dominated the others. "Serena! Shut the front door. You've left it wide open."

Serena turned and ran headlong toward the door heedless of the snow that came in over the sides of her loafers. She slammed it, paddled back to the car, and jumped in beside Alice. An instant later Mr. Bruce let in the clutch and they drove off. "Just as well you decided against walking," he said. "You wouldn't have reached the church until after the service."

"I'm sorry I kept you waiting," Squeak began. "I think maybe I must have been half asleep——"

"Half asleep!" Johnny giggled. "You were sound asleep. Snoring almost. With a book going up and down on your tummy."

Mrs. Hilsen and Alice laughed. Squeak said nothing, but now crossness, in which sleepiness, and feeling like a fool were all unpleasantly mixed, shook her like a chill. "You were awful, awful sound asleep," Johnny went on. Alice stopped laughing and craned her neck to look at him.

"When did you wake her?" she asked. "When Mum first told you or later on when you happened to remember it?"

"Well," Johnny began, and Squeak could hear him shifting around behind her. "Well," he said, "she said she was going to walk . . ."

"Johnny is the youngest!" Mrs. Hilsen broke in. "In Norway a girl of sixteen would be expected to dress her little brother and be ready on time herself. When I was sixteen I could weave and spin . . ."

At that moment Mr. Bruce brought the car to a stop in front of Mrs. Hilsen's immaculately neat little house on East Linden Street and in the flurry of good-bys, good nights, and Christmas greetings she never finished her sentence.

They drove on the short distance up the ridge and as they turned in at the Episcopal Church the new snow packed heavily under the car wheels. Mr. Bruce grunted. "If we have any more snow tonight the driving will be grim!"

Mrs. Bruce smiled up at her husband as she jumped out of the car. "If anybody can manage it you can," she said. As she caught sight of Squeak her smile faded. "Serena. Loafers! In this snow. And your hat is filthy. Why couldn't you get your clothes ready first instead of all that talk about walking? Honestly, you're so changeable it's hard sometimes to know whether you're sixteen or six!"

She brushed Squeak's hat and reached out to brush off her coat collar when Mr. Bruce took her arm. "Come on, darling," he said. "After all, this is Christmas Eve and the last time Sunny'll be singing in the choir for we don't know how long. I don't want to miss even the opening chord of the processional."

They moved on into the church, which was already well filled, brilliantly lit, and heady with the mixed fragrance of balsam pine, and candle wax. Squeak started to catch up with Johnny, who usually turned shy as they reached the church and held her hand, but tonight he pulled off his cap without being told, shoved his hand into Alice's, and the two of them followed their parents while Squeak struggled to get some of the snow off her loafers on the inside mat.

The choir had left the robing room by this time and was forming in line along the small side aisle. Squeak straightened up and saw that Sunny was looking at her. "Poor Squeak." Sunny's lips formed the words soundlessly as she nodded at Squeak's shoes. "Poor Squeak!"

Squeak smiled back and, still uncomfortably aware of her cold wet feet, paddled down to the family pew just as the music started.

Darling Sunny, Squeak thought as she knelt beside Johnny. She's the only one in the family who can be sorry for people without blaming them first. Squeak gulped with her head bowed and now it swept over her in a great organ-borne burst of feeling what it was going to mean to have Sunny married and living away from home.

They stood up for the processional and Squeak caught sight of Charlie Reed standing straight and stiff at the end of his family's pew, with eyes for no one but Sunny. She looked away and her mind swept back to something Sunny had said one evening last summer when she had come upstairs to Squeak's room to tell her about her engagement. "But how do you know?" Squeak had asked, thinking of all the other boys and men who had been in love with Sunny. "How do you know that you will like him, love him, better than everybody, not just now, but always?"

And Sunny had answered, her face and her voice radiant with happiness. "Someday the right man will come for you, Squeak, and then if you've waited and trusted you'll know, darling, you'll know."

The hymn was over and as Squeak kneeled again the remembered words rang in her ear. "You'll know, darling, you'll know." Squeak's heart lifted and she shut her eyes, conjuring up the hero, the very perfect gentle knight, of "The Idyll." She saw him instantly and smiled a proud, secret little smile into her folded hands. The family could say all they liked about her being changeable and fickle. In a way, perhaps, it was true, but to her dream, her beau ideal, she was constant.

2

O Holy Night Squeak went on thinking about "The Idyll" until the congregation rose for the reading of the psalm and Johnny pushed up against her. "You help me," he whispered. "You're a good place finder."

Squeak turned to the fiftieth psalm and they read together, " 'Out of Sion hath God appeared, in perfect beauty.' "

She heard Johnny's small voice mumbling the words and just beyond him her mother's voice and Alice's. The Rev. Mr. Parker read the third verse. As the congregation began on the fourth Squeak heard an unfamiliar woman's voice behind her. She straightened up suddenly, stirred by the exceptional quality of the woman's voice and accent. At the sixth verse Johnny prodded her and she went on pointing out the words to him, but she no longer read aloud herself, too intent on hearing, on straining out from the rumble of muttered reading the keen unexpected beauty of the perfect speech behind her.

As the congregation sat down again Squeak craned her neck, trying to see who had been speaking. She caught a glimpse of dark fur, and two pews farther back and to her left a flash of carrot-red hair. The hair belonged to Cliff Hawks, and as soon as he saw Squeak looking at him he began to make faces as though he were Johnny's age instead of eighteen. Squeak straightened instantly and as she did so saw that Alice had also been looking behind her. "Cliff the Hawk in *church!*" Alice whispered. Her eyebrows arched upward and Squeak very nearly laughed out loud.

Somehow she managed to keep a straight face. A moment later the congregation rose to recite the creed. Once more she heard the beautiful voice behind her and listened spellbound. She didn't dare look back a second time during the service, but as soon as the whole thing was over she turned to see who had been speaking.

She recognized old Mrs. Apsley and a few other neighbors. Beyond that she saw a plump, bald man, whom she didn't know. Beside him was a lady in a dark mink coat who, Squeak realized, must be the possessor of the glorious speaking voice. For an instant Squeak felt flat with astonishment. After that voice she had expected someone tall and young and blondly beautiful, like Sunny. This woman might be forty, almost Mum's age, and she was as small and dark and slight as Squeak herself.

"Let's go!" Johnny crowded past her in the aisle. "Let's hurry."

Usually Squeak hated the insipid, long drawn-out after-church chatter, but tonight she was so interested in the lady in the mink coat that she didn't notice that it took even longer than usual to get out of church. It was only when she reached the damp, crowded vestibule that she realized that half the congregation was still inside and that there must be a block ahead. Mr. Bruce made his way over to her and she saw that Johnny was with him. "You stay by the door while I try and get the car," he said. "It's been snowing hard again and half the cars in town are stuck on the driveway. Mum's coming with me."

Squeak and Johnny moved outside and joined a crowd which included Sunny, Charlie Reed, Tom Connaught, and half a dozen others. No cars passed the church and the snow muffled the noise of horns and motors from the parking place at the rear. For a moment there was only the sound of voices, the creak of the church door, and crunching footsteps. Then, from across the village green, Squeak caught the jingle of sleigh bells. The sound grew stronger and as a horse-drawn sleigh pulled up by the church Squeak saw that Jube Carter was driving. "Come on, Sunny," he shouted. "Alice! You, Tom. Hurry."

The crowd dashed off toward the sleigh and the older people left by the church door smiled appreciatively. "Have a good time!" someone said.

"It looks just like a Christmas card."

"Like old times."

"Have a lovely——"

Just then Squeak saw Cliff Hawks push his way forward and heard him shout, "Hey, Jube. Wait! Let me go with you."

They'll never take him, Squeak thought; Alice said it was only the college-age crowd and up! For an instant it looked as though Squeak was right, and then as Cliff gestured with a long envelope he held in his hand Jube shrugged and let him climb on board. It's mean, it isn't fair, Squeak thought. If Cliff can go why can't I? Just then she was aware that someone had patted her shoulder, and turned to find that old Mrs. Apsley was saying, "Why aren't you going, little Serena? They look as though they were going to have such a happy time."

Before Squeak could answer Mrs. Apsley darted away, and her heart sank. Mrs. Apsley invariably butted into other people's business and she was perfectly capable of calling out to Jube to come back for "little Serena" right in front of everyone.

"I promised Mum I'd go home with her," Squeak began, but then she saw that Mrs. Apsley had already forgotten her and was introducing herself to a tall distinguished-looking stranger who had just come out of the church.

Squeak moved a safe distance away from Mrs. Apsley and looked back at the sleigh. It's not fair, she thought. Cliff's younger than any of them. It's like the time ages ago when Mum asked him over to my picnic and he wouldn't play with anyone but Alice because he said the rest of us were babies. And he's nearer my age than Alice's!

The sleigh bells jingled louder than ever as Jube drove off. Cliff turned and waved and Squeak grabbed Johnny's arm. "Let's get out of here," was all she said out loud, but inwardly she felt like screaming with envy. "Let's find Mum and Dad."

They started across the snow to the parking lot and saw that the cars were in a hopeless tangle. Tires skidded, bumpers locked, and not one car passed through. "Some mess!" Johnny said, and a moment later they both saw Mr. Bruce striding up the little hill toward them.

"I'm going to get sand at the rectory," he called out. "Better wait inside the church."

"I'll come with you!" Johnny shouted, and ran forward and caught his father's hand. Squeak started after him, but, when her loafer nearly stuck in the snow at the first step, changed her mind. Her feet were so cold and wet that they had contracted and if she tried to hurry she'd end up walking through the snow in stocking feet.

She started back to the church, but when she found the vestibule was crowded with elderly people changed her mind. Right now she was in no mood for Mrs. Apsley's brand of questions and pity, so she turned to the left and moved cautiously along the outside wall of the church away from the parking lot. The masonry jutted out just beyond her and she knew if she rounded the jut she would have both privacy and shelter from the wind.

By the time she rounded the corner the fitful gust of snow was over and as she stopped to brush herself off by the light from one of the church windows she saw that she was not alone. The lady in the mink coat came forward with her hand out. "So you escaped the gossip's gallery too?" she said. "An old lady who introduced herself as Mrs. Apsley talked so much that I ducked back here!"

"Me too!" Squeak almost stepped out of her loafers again as she shook hands. "She's a horror."

The lady laughed, and the sound was as intriguing in its own way as her voice. "Good luck our both landing here, because I was looking for you in the first place. You are Serena Bruce, aren't you?"

"Yes. But I'm afraid I don't know your name."

"Of course you don't. Stupid of me not to think of it. I'm Clare Clayton and I'm living at Holly House. I inherited the place when Cousin Dorothea Frostgate died. I've just come back from living in England."

"So you're the cousin no one in the village has met. How perfectly wonderful that it's you!"

"Why?" The single word was as light as a feathered arrow, but Squeak felt her neck redden under the scratchy wool of her coat. For an instant she hesitated, and then as usual spoke before she thought out what she really wanted to say.

"Well, you see, I just love Holly House. I liked Mrs. Frostgate a lot and I used to go down there all the time. Alone, I mean, and not with the rest of the family. I'm glad somebody nice is living there."

Clare Clayton laughed a soft, smoky little sound that was oddly encouraging. "And you think I'm nice. I'm very glad to hear it. I'm not so sure that the rest of the neighbors think I'm the right person to have inherited Holly House."

"But of course you are!" Squeak was so in earnest she stopped feeling self-conscious. "Mrs. Frostgate loved voices, speaking voices, that is, better than almost anything. She almost got me to take elocution lessons once and your voice is just the kind of thing she was talking about. I heard you in church just now and nearly broke my neck trying to see who you were. You're the perfect person to have inherited Holly House."

" 'She brought him butter on a lordly dish!' " Mrs. Clayton quoted. "Bless the girl." Her voice was still offhand and joking, but her face, as she turned into the light from the narrow church window, looked radiant and young with pleasure.

Squeak started to say something, but at that moment she saw one car followed by another and another reach the road beyond them and knew that the sand must be working on the hill behind the church. "Jeepers," she said. "Mum and Dad'll scalp me. They're sure to have gotten the car started by this time." She started to go back the way she had come, then, realizing it would be quicker to go down around the church by the old, abandoned carriage shed, turned in her tracks. "This way is shorter," she said, scrunching up her toes to keep on her shoes. "Either way we'll get snowy."

"Lead on, Macduff!" Mrs. Clayton was only a step behind her. "A friend of mine took me out to dinner and I forced him to go to the carol service. He has to drive down to New York after he's left me home, so he won't appreciate waiting either."

Squeak plowed on feeling comfortably conspiratorial. As she made the corner into the valley she stopped short and stared at the view below her. The moon had come out again while they were talking, and had turned the room of the little shed silver, while the north wall which was in shadow seemed ebony black. The shed must have been used earlier in the evening, because an old-fashioned oil lamp hung from the rafters and sent out a single golden beam through the small window.

27

"Look," Squeak got out, and in that instant she ached with the need for words to express such beauty. "Golly!"

Clare Clayton stood motionless for a moment. As a car horn honked in the distance she moved on again and sighed. "It is quite perfect," she said quietly. "I—I wish all the people in the world who aren't sure that Christmas really happened could see that—and know."

They went on without speaking and as they passed in the lee of the shed they saw the cars crawling out over the newly spread sand.

"Mark. Mark! Here I am," Clare Clayton called, and without as much as a backward glance at Squeak ran forward toward a black Cadillac car. She was halfway toward it when a tall man with his coat collar turned up jumped out of the car behind the Cadillac and ran toward her.

"Clare! Wait!" he called out. "I must speak to you."

Clare Clayton stopped short, while a few feet behind her Squeak gaped with surprise. Clare Clayton looked the man up and down, and then with her head high moved on toward the Cadillac. "Please get out of my way," she said, and her voice, which Squeak had just found moving, reverent, and humorous by turns, was hard as steel.

The man put out his hands as though to stop her, but she avoided him and reached the Cadillac just as the bald man with whom she had been at church pushed open the door. "I knew you'd seen him!" the bald man said furiously. "Honestly, Clare, of all the rotten tricks!"

Squeak never heard Clare's answer because as soon as the car door shut the driver started off. She stared after the car in bewilderment. As she turned away she saw the tall man who had accosted Clare drop his hands disconsolately and walk back to his own car.

He's the same one Mrs. Apsley spoke to, she thought, and at that moment she heard her mother's voice. "Squeak! Squeak, we're right over here!"

Squeak ran forward and as her mother slid over to make room for her she gave Squeak's shoulder a quick affectionate squeeze. "You must be frozen, darling. Really frozen."

"Only my feet," Squeak said, and suddenly it seemed good to be with the family again. "And they'll thaw out in no time."

"Mum, did you see that horse sled?" Johnny asked, and went on in the same breath. "Boy, I'm hungry! I'll bet I can eat a hundred of Mrs. Hilsen's Kringle cookies."

"I'm going to make some hot chocolate to go with them," Mrs. Bruce said. "The frothy kind with marshmallow on top that Squeak likes."

"Good," Squeak said. "Terrific. I bet the girls don't get anything nearly as good as that at the Carters'."

They had reached home by this time and now as they hurried toward the house Mother beamed at her. "You're a good sport, lambie. I'm afraid this Christmas is a little flat for you with all of us thinking more about Sunny's wedding than anything else."

"I like it," Squeak said. She crossed the kitchen floor which felt deliciously warm and smooth under her bare feet. "I like it a lot. And listen, Mum and Dad, you know what? I met the woman—lady—who inherited Holly House and she's fascinating."

"She's got beautiful clothes." Mrs. Bruce measured, mixed, and stirred with expert motions. "Mrs. Apsley pointed her out to me as we were leaving church."

"And the most marvelous voice," Squeak began, but just then Johnny came in demanding help with rubber boots and Mum pointed out that the kitchen table wasn't the right place for Squeak's coat and muffler.

Finally when everything was put away and they were drinking their hot chocolate in front of the fire she tried again. "What else do you know about Miss, or is it Mrs., Clayton?" she asked. "You haven't met her, have you?"

"She's Mrs.," Mr. Bruce said. "Seems to me she was married to some actor chap who was killed during the war. And I think she was on the stage herself."

"An actress!" Squeak said. "How terrific! Did you ever see her act?"

"Never," Mum said, "but we'll ask Grandpa about her when he comes up here tomorrow for Christmas dinner. He knows the names and roles of every actress who's played in New York in the last fifty years."

"Is she old?" Squeak's face fell. "Really old?"

Both Mum and Dad laughed and soon Squeak laughed with them.

"Breaking up," Mum said. "Thirty-five to forty, to look at her, but she might be forty-five like me and be actually senile."

Just then Johnny yawned. "I've eaten six Kringles," he said, "and drunk so much hot chocolate my feet feel dizzy. Boy, I wish it was tomorrow."

Mrs. Bruce took him off to bed. Squeak and her father put away the dishes and Squeak went upstairs and started to undress, still thinking over the evening. It was queer the way Clare Clayton had brushed off that tall, good-looking man and made the bald one so angry, but perhaps it wasn't very important. Not as important as her voice, or her laughter, anyway, that made you feel witty and bright and sensitive by turns as you listened to it.

Squeak pulled on her nightgown, and then another and entrancing thought struck her. Now that there was an actress living at Holly House she, Serena Bruce, would learn how to act herself.

It was foreordained, "meant," as Mrs. Hilsen said about anything that simply had to happen, and the only queer thing about it was that she hadn't thought of it before except once for a week or so the first season that the Vagabond Players brought summer stock to Stapleton.

She saw her underclothes on the floor and as she stooped to pick them up swept into a deep bow as though she were lifting up flowers from an imaginary stage. "Thank you," she whispered, and blew kisses to an audience. "Thank you, dear friends."

A moment later she dropped the underclothes on a chair and turned to open the window. The cold air was sobering and Squeak stopped acting as she looked out. She saw the light in the barn that had been left on for Sunny and Alice and it reminded her of the moment behind the church when she and Clare Clayton had looked down at the small, snowbound shed.

She scurried across her room, found the Donne where it had dropped on the floor, picked it up, and began reading in bed. The book opened to passages that Alice had marked and that Squeak had read before church. "No man is an iland entire to himself," and further on, "God emploies several translators," and "God's hand is in every translation." Squeak read the passage over twice, turned out the lights, and gave a sigh of satisfaction as she slid further under the covers. John Donne might have been writing about this very evening. Clare Clayton had been fascinating, challenging, frightening by turns, but when she had looked down at the shed and had seen in it the stable in Bethlehem she had been God's translator.

Squeak lay very still smiling up at the dark ceiling. She felt happy and relaxed and gloriously free to conjure up long, golden fancies. Not "The Idyll," this time, but the theater, which glowed with a welcoming light now that she was certain that Clare Clayton would be her teacher, her guide.

Squeak stretched, and as she rolled over onto her side heard Mum and Dad's voices downstairs and guessed that they were filling stockings. She heard Mum say, "Look, Jack! Don't you think Johnny'll love this monkey?" and Dad's deep laugh.

For a few minutes there was no sound except the light, cold whistle of the wind outside, and then Dad began to sing, " 'Oh holy night, the stars were brightly shining . . .' " The familiar words carried softly up the stairs. Squeak smiled to herself and fell asleep.

3

Christmas Day in the Morning "Wake up!" "Merry Christmas.
Do get up, Squeak!" Squeak heard Johnny's feet scudding down
the hall and a moment later he burst into her room, his round face
rosy with excitement. "Mum's awake, Dad's awake, both the girls,
and we're waiting for you for stockings."

Squeak shut her eyes again and as she sniffed the mixed fragrance
of coffee and balsam tried to remember what made this Christmas
morning different from any other. Was it Sunny? Sunny's wedding?
"The snow's melting," Johnny said, and then Squeak remembered.
Last night outside the church. Mrs. Clayton. And herself on the
stage! She kicked off the blankets and gestured to Johnny to leave.
"Avaunt, base carl. I do not require thy services."

Johnny stuck his neck out so he looked like a startled turtle.
"*What?* What you saying, Squeak?"

She pushed down the window and turned on him. "Don't call
me Squeak," she said, and found her teeth were chattering. "Call
me Serena."

"O.K.," Johnny said, and stationed himself in front of her bed
so that she couldn't get back under the covers. "But hurry, Sque—I
mean—Serena. I've been waiting for my stocking for ages."

Squeak pulled on her wrapper and shoved her feet into woolly
slippers while Johnny went on talking. "I've got a super present

for you. Two presents, really, and I paid for 'em with my own money out of the piggy bank."

She turned from brushing her hair and saw that he had his hands clasped tightly together in front of his chest in a habit he had had as a baby and had never entirely outgrown. Once Dad had called it his "angel stance" and right now with his light hair fanning out from the back of his head like a bristling halo he looked exactly like a Christmas angel. "I'm ready. Merry Christmas," Squeak said, and he turned and flew down the hall.

"I've got her!" he yelled, and all angelicness disappeared in a tornado of small-boy excitement. "Mum. Dad. Alice. Sunny! I've got Squeak and when can I have my stocking?"

"Right now, darling," Mrs. Bruce said, and Squeak saw that she and Alice were all dressed while Dad and Sunny, like herself, were still in their bathrobes. "Come on in, Squeak honey. Your stocking's over there. Alice, give Dad his stocking or he'll go to sleep again right in our faces."

Mr. Bruce made a pathetic face and everyone except Johnny, who was digging into his own stocking like an excited terrier, laughed. "I like stockings," Dad said. "I love stockings, but I think it's cruel and inhuman treatment not to let me shave and have my coffee first."

"Stockings first, coffee second," Mum said, and began opening her own. "Have you no soul for tradition?"

Squeak grinned to herself and for a minute she forgot to act anything at all. This was Christmas all right. The pine smell, the knobby stockings, all of them clustered around Mum and Dad's beds with Mum all dressed and Dad in pajamas pretending to be desperate for his breakfast. She picked up the candy cane that hung on top of her stocking and lifted out a flat red pincushion. Beneath that was a box of bobby pins and a Yo-yo. "I got one too!"

Johnny shouted, and began tossing his Yo-yo directly in front of her. "And jeepers, it makes sparks. Try yours, Squeakie. Try it!"

Squeak had already tightened the string of her Yo-yo, but as she heard the irritating nickname she put it down. Squeakie. A Yo-yo. A babyish nickname and a child's toy for a person about to go on the stage? She smiled distantly and when she spoke her voice was old enough for Whistler's mother. "You're very clever with it, Johnny darling. Very clever."

"Huh?" Johnny gave her a puzzled stare before he dove back into his stocking and pulled out a small woolly monkey. Alice, who had been watching, reached out for Johnny's Yo-yo. "Look," she said, and swung it skillfully. "I can make it spank the baby."

Squeak pretended not to see her and went on opening her own stocking. A box of stuffed dates, a carved dog for her whatnot collection, and a small stapler. "These are really handy," Dad said as he took a stapler out of his own sock. "And now Squeak and I'll each have one when she comes and works for me in the advertising business."

"But I'm not going into the ad——" Squeak began, but just then the telephone rang and as Sunny hurried past her she had no chance to finish her sentence.

"Oh, I'm sure that's Charlie!" Sunny said. "He promised he'd call up first thing in the morning."

Squeak turned back to her stocking and found a small manicure set in the toe. She had never bothered much about her nails and for an instant she was as disappointed as though she had been Johnny's age and had found a piece of pumice stone. Then she remembered it was just the right thing for an actress and held it out with an arched, exaggerated motion of her wrist.

"It seemed sort of a mean trick, putting in a hint like that," Mum said. "But with Sunny's wedding coming up we had to stick mostly

35

to useful presents and Dad and I both thought the case was pretty."

"It's divine, it's *enchawnting*," Squeak said, but as she brought out the unaccustomed broad *A* her voice soared into one of the little squeaks which had given her her nickname, and she blushed furiously.

"I'm glad you like it." Mum spoke unusually quickly. "And I hope you'll find it useful."

"Oh, I'm sure I shall," Squeak said. "You see, I've decided I'm not going to be a copy writer or—or—a writer of any kind. I'm going on the stage. When I'm through school, of course."

Alice let out a yelp of laughter, and Squeak turned on her. "What's so funny about that? Nobody howled when you said last fall you were going to be a biologist."

"That's different," Alice said. "I'm at college and it's time I chose a career and besides I haven't been saying I was going to be this, that, and the other thing every two months all my life. I've always been interested——"

At that moment Dad hauled himself out of bed and began shooing both girls toward the door. "Beat it," he said. "Scram. I can take stocking before breakfast because it's Christmas, but not careers. Any of you can be anything you feel you are really cut out to be, but I can't talk about it until I've had orange juice, two eggs, bacon, and coffee. Loads of coffee."

They heard him turn on the shower as they moved into the hall. Johnny tugged on Squeak's wrapper. "Dad dresses awful fast when he's hungry," he said. "But we'll have to wait to go into the library until you're ready too, so won't you hurry?"

Squeak practiced acting by giving him a smile like a tired but indulgent aunt, and then Sunny came back from the telephone. "It was Charlie!" she said. "And he said to say Merry Christmas to all of you and he'll be over later on in the morning."

"Sunny, listen." Squeak moved forward to tell her about becoming an actress, but Sunny had already gone down the hall into her own room and Squeak could hear her telling Alice all over again that it was Charlie who had called. They don't care about me, Squeak thought, and went up to her own room to dress. They don't understand. Not one of them. Or perhaps they're waiting to argue me out of it. Just let them try!

She came downstairs after the others, but nobody said anything about her being late. She drank her orange juice waiting for someone to challenge her great decision, but instead the girls went right on talking about the party the night before. "The sleigh ride was the best part of it," Alice said, and Sunny nodded.

"Much," she said. "I kept wishing Charlie and I were home here and I think everyone else felt the same way. When Charlie gets out of the Army and we have a house of our own we're always going to stay home on Christmas Eve." Her eyes looked dreamy the way they always did when she spoke of the rainbow days ahead when Charlie would be out of the Army, and then Alice spoke.

"Cliff Hawks didn't want to stay home," she said. "He'd use other people's Christmas spirit or anything else to get himself invited to a party."

"Remember he hasn't a real home to go to," Mr. Bruce began as Squeak leaned toward Alice.

"I thought he asked himself!" she said. "I saw him run out and argue with Jube, and then when he held up something Jube let him come."

"That was a letter for you, as a matter of fact," Alice said. "That he was delivering for somebody else, but of course he couldn't think of giving it to Mum or Dad to give to you when it gave him a chance to horn in on a Christmas party."

"For me?" Serena said. "From whom? What is it?"

"Wait and see," Alice said, and just then Johnny succeeded in getting his father up from the breakfast table. "Let's go," he shouted. "Smallest first and that's me. Into the library to open presents."

They all followed him at once and Squeak headed straight for the wing chair which had held her presents ever since the first Christmas she could remember, when it had been half covered by an oversized Teddy bear.

"Boy. Oh *boy*. It's a cowboy suit. And listen to my claxon-bell noise maker!" Johnny shouted.

"Jack, darling!"

Squeak rummaged past the parcels tied with tags in the family's familiar handwritings until she came to an envelope addressed to Miss Serena Talbot Bruce, kindness of Clifford Hawks, in a hand she had never seen before. She tore it open and saw that the letter was signed by Clare Clayton. "Dear Serena," she began and now she was so intrigued that even the noise Johnny was making with his new patented "claxon-bell" seemed far away.

A few weeks ago I found a letter in Cousin Dorothea Frostgate's desk telling me that she wanted you and Clifford Hawks to have her books after her death. I would have communicated with you both at once about this, but first I had to clear it with the lawyers and appraisers, as the letter was not a regulation part of her will. This has just been done and I have also spoken over the telephone to your parents, who seem to have no objection to your receiving a present which I am afraid is going to entail a good deal of work. I have spoken to Cliff Hawks, who has promised that you will receive this in time for Christmas, but I hope to meet you very soon myself. In the last few years while I have been living abroad every letter I received from Cousin Dorothea mentioned you with the greatest affection.

Sincerely,

Clare Clayton

For a second Squeak's eyelids pricked and her hand shook. She remembered, as though it had happened that morning, the day, over two years ago, when Mrs. Frostgate had taken her out to the barn, pointed out the two cases of her late husband's books that were stored there, and told her that someday they would be hers. She had been thrilled at the time, and then had forgotten it, but old Mrs. Frostgate had remembered.

"Mum. Dad. Everybody. Look!" she said, and waved the letter. "It's about Mrs. Frostgate's books."

The two girls read the letter together while Johnny demanded to know what it was all about. "I'm glad you met Mrs. Clayton last night," Dad said. "I only saw her to nod to, but both Mum and I thought she sounded terribly nice when she telephoned about your having the books. You see, legally she isn't obligated to let you have them at all."

"Of course it'll be a nuisance off her hands," Mum put in, "but she was nice about that, too. I wish I'd thought to ask her about helping with the Community Chest drive."

"I think it's perfectly fascinating," Sunny said, and turned back to her own presents. "And darling of Mrs. Frostgate."

Alice handed the letter back to Squeak and her eyebrows lifted. "Rather you than me, Squeakie," she said. "Working in close co-operation with Cliff the Hawk wouldn't be my idea of bliss."

"It would be his," Sunny said. "Last night Jube let him come because he said he had a message for one of the Bruces. Jube thought it was Alice or me and he was quite cross when he found out Cliff had been a little tricky to be near Alice."

"I should think he would be!" Squeak said. "Cliff's a mess."

Just then they heard Charlie Reed's voice at the door and as Sunny flew to let him in Johnny came over to Serena. "Open my present," he pleaded. "You've just got to."

39

She picked up a small, squashed, and unmistakably Johnny-wrapped present, but long before she could untie the string he told her what was inside. "It's a notebook and a Rudolph the Red-nosed Reindeer pencil," he said. "And they cost thirty-five cents!"

"They're super," Squeak said. "Thanks a million."

Johnny beamed. "I thought you'd like 'em," he said. "They're for you to use when you're being a writer, just the way my cowboy suit and pistol are for me to use when I'm being a cowboy."

"But I'm not going——" Squeak began, thought better of it, and gave Johnny a hug instead. She started to open a square parcel with "Love from Dad" on it, and realized that he was standing beside her. "I don't know," he said as she tore open the paper. "I'm just not sure——"

Squeak looked down at the Roget's *Thesaurus*, Hammond's *Nature Atlas of America* and the worn little copy of Tennyson's *Idylls of the King*. Her heart turned over, wondering if by any possible chance he had guessed about her daydream. She had never read as much as a word of the book; it was only the name, the single glamorous word *"Idyll"* that had charmed her. "I just threw in the Tennyson," Dad said. "Belonged to my father when he was at college."

Squeak breathed more deeply. So he hadn't guessed. She dropped the books and was just going to throw her arms around Dad's neck when Alice's laugh stopped her like a slap in the face. "You certainly guessed wrong that time, Pop," she said. "Reference books for an actress. Well, anyway I'll be glad to borrow them."

Squeak choked. "Not on your life," she said, and Alice's eyebrows arched upward as they always did when she was teasing.

"Changed your mind again?" she said. "What are you going to be now, a lexicographer or a snake charmer? They'd be handy for that."

Squeak hesitated, torn between not hurting Dad's feelings and convincing him that she had really meant it about being an actress. "Thanks a lot," she said, but by the time she had the words out Dad was already piling up all the used wrappings and she couldn't see his face. "They—they're just what I wanted."

4

Target   At four o'clock on Christmas afternoon Squeak started off for Holly House to talk to Mrs. Clayton about the books and, what was much more important, about going on the stage. The family had been maddening about her decision to be an actress, but now, as she tramped along the deserted road, that hardly seemed to matter. Great artists were always misunderstood at home.

Squeak smiled and conjured up such a rosy future for herself that she hardly noticed the cold, wet drizzle. She was in the star's dressing room after a triumphant first night. The hero, the nameless knight of "The Idyll," was there in beautifully tailored evening clothes, waiting to take her off to a champagne supper at the Diamond Swan. Beside him were a dozen equally handsome, superbly dressed admirers, and Alice, who was still wearing her old gray suit and shabby loafers. "I always knew my sister would be a success," Alice said. "Why, when she was only sixteen it was perfectly clear she was a dedicated actress."

Squeak walked on, heedless of the icy slush, while the dream Serena smiled graciously, forgivingly, and motioned to her maid to lend Miss Alice an evening dress and the extra mink wrap. "Dear Alice." The real Squeak's lips moved, she was so engrossed with her daydream. "I seem to remember your joking about my being a snake charmer."

Alice scowled and the hero sprang forward and brushed Serena's fingers with his lips. "You could charm anything, my dearest," he said. "Now come and dance with me."

Just then a large blob of melting snow blew off a tree and trickled down Squeak's neck. She shivered and the daydream disappeared for good. She passed the snowy lions looking wet and naked in the light rain, and remembered uncomfortably that always before at Christmas time Pat Dugan, old Mrs. Frostgate's chauffeur and handy man, had decorated them with gay holly collars.

Squeak walked on and now she thought of the hot, steamy September day, shortly after Mrs. Frostgate's death, when she had determined to decorate the lions alone. The mental picture of herself coming out on a cold, dark Christmas Eve with no one but ghosts and memories for company had been so vivid that she had told the two elder girls all about it. "What a darling thought," Sunny had said. "It reminds me of a story I read once, was it called *Memorial for the Dead?*"

"You mean Henry James' *Altar of the Dead?*" Alice had said. "Well, I can't say that would remind me of decorating Mrs. Frostgate's lions, but perhaps I'm just not the sensitive type. I thought that story dripped!"

Squeak had determined to read the story at once, but she never remembered to take the book out of the library and hadn't thought about the lions again until this minute. The only lucky thing was that the girls had forgotten too, or Alice would have teased her unmercifully.

At that moment she reached the front door and rang the bell, expecting a butler or perhaps a parlormaid in a frilly uniform, like the servant in one of the summer-stock plays last summer. She leaned forward, practicing a polite but dignified smile, and decided that she would tell whoever answered the door that Miss Serena Talbot-Bruce was calling on Mrs. Clayton.

At that moment the door opened and as Squeak saw that Miss Petersen, Mrs. Hilsen's elder sister, had opened it, the smile froze on her lips. Miss Petersen worked for many of the same families as her sister and disapproved of all of them. Right now she looked as though she disapproved of Squeak most of all and when she spoke she sounded it. "Vell, Sqveak," she said. "Are you coming in or should I freeze myself vaiting?"

"Sorry," Squeak said, and scuttled through the doorway. "Merry Christmas, Miss Petersen, and could I see Mrs. Clayton, or is she resting?"

Miss Petersen's sniff was dynamic. "She sleeps until noon, and then argues with a gentleman caller over sherry until nearly two and from that she should rest?" She started for the kitchen, and then called back over her shoulder. "Mrs. Clayton? That Bruce girl, Sqveak, to see you."

As the door slammed behind her Squeak stood uncertainly in the silent, golden oak hall. In the old days Anna Dugan, Pat's wife, would have let her in, covered her with Irish hugs and compliments, and sent her on her way rejoicing toward the library, where old Mrs. Frostgate's loud, jolly voice would already be shouting, "Serena, honeybunch, is that you? Tell Anna to tell Margaret to send you up some of the chocolate cake." Now there was only the last echo of Miss Petersen's footsteps, and then silence in the old house that had always been alive with the song of half a dozen canaries, a parrot, Irish voices, and, loudest and most cheerful of all, old Mrs. Frostgate herself.

Serena took a step forward and the creak of her ski boot sounded like an explosion. She took another step, glad that Miss Petersen hadn't noticed how much mud she was trailing in. Suddenly Mrs.

Clayton's voice sounded so close beside her that she jumped. "Hello, Serena," she said. "What a nice surprise."

Mrs. Clayton stood by the side door to the drawing room which Mrs. Frostgate never used, and beckoned to Serena to join her. "Come on in," she said. "It's a little like a mausoleum, but I'm trying to get a fire going to cheer it up for this evening. A party of old friends are driving down from Lenox to have dinner with me and I don't want them to have to sit looking at empty shelves in the library."

As Squeak stepped forward her heart beat faster. Friends down from Lenox and up from New York. A gentleman caller for sherry. That was all part of the theater, the wonderful glamorous world which would soon be her own. She was out of the hall now and in the big cold drawing room, which was lit from a large, hideously ugly ceiling light. She blinked at the brightness, and then, when she really saw Clare Clayton, blinked again. Last night she had only seen Clare in church and in the moonlight. After her first surprise over Clare's age she had been so impressed by her voice and the aura of good fur and expensive perfume that she hadn't really noticed details of her clothes. What she had expected now she wasn't quite sure. Perhaps black velvet slacks, a sequin shirt, and a long onyx holder for imported cigarettes. Instead the slight, dark-haired woman in front of her was dressed in faded blue jeans, a checked shirt, and she wasn't smoking at all, but chewing furiously.

She must have noticed Squeak staring at her mouth, because she laughed, and with a gesture that reminded Squeak of Johnny, twisted a small paper box out of her pocket and offered it politely. "Have a Jujube?" she said. "They're horrid little things, but I'm chewing them like mad because I've just given up smoking and miss it fiendishly."

"Dad gave it up for a month last year and it nearly killed him,"

Squeak said. "He said he was doing it as penance for writing copy for the Capitol Cigarette Company."

Mrs. Clayton laughed and the sound made Squeak feel so witty that she stopped being disappointed by the clothes that looked like Mum's on cleaning day. "I have fallen for your father," Mrs. Clayton said. "I knew I liked his voice over the telephone and the penance idea is heavenly."

"Dad said the same thing about you! About liking your voice, I mean, and then he told me about your being on the stage and your husband being killed——"

"He told you what?" Mrs. Clayton interrupted and now there was an edge to her voice that left Squeak quaking.

"I'm sorry," she muttered. "I didn't mean to be dumb. Mrs. Frostgate never let anyone mention her son who was killed in the First World War."

"It isn't that!" Mrs. Clayton said, and as Squeak looked up in surprise she seemed to have grown taller and appallingly remote. "I love talking about Basil. I went to England especially to be near the people he'd been with last. It's about my being in the theater. What did your father say about that?"

"He didn't say much. He didn't even know what plays you'd been in or anything. I think he'd just heard in his office in New York that you were an actress."

"People don't know about it here, then?" Clare Clayton sounded relieved. "In the village, I mean. I don't even like to have people discuss me in connection with the theater."

"I'm sure they don't," Squeak said. "And I promise I'll never say anything about it, and you know Dad really didn't know or say much at all. In fact Mum suggested that we ask Gramps, that's my grandfather, Dr. Lawrence, about you, because he's seen every play in New York for the past fifty years."

46

"Putting me tidily in a bracket with the late lamented Lillian Russell," Mrs. Clayton said sharply. Serena felt a hot, embarrassed red sweep up over her own face and neck. Mrs. Clayton saw it and put out her hand impulsively.

"I'm sorry, Serena," she said. "I wasn't trying to be mean. It's simply that one of the reasons why I'm living up here, besides getting the place ready to sell, is to stay away from the theater. I haven't been in anything since the year Basil was killed and right now I don't even want to think about the theater. I need whatever brains I've got to straighten out the Chinese puzzle of Cousin Dorothea's estate."

"And then you're going to move?" Squeak said, and in spite of the fact that Mrs. Clayton was thrilling, disappointing, and terrifying by turns she was truly sorry. "I—I wish you wouldn't."

Clare Clayton gave Squeak's hand a quick squeeze. "You lamb," she said. "I'm not moving far. Only into the cottage where Pat and Anna Dugan used to live. That and your books and the birds which were left to Anna are about the only things that aren't mortgaged up to the hilt. And now I suppose you want to know more about why I wrote you that letter?"

"Oh yes. Thank you, Mrs. Clayton——" Squeak began as the telephone rang in the next room.

Clare Clayton grimaced as she went off to answer it, and then called back over her shoulder. "Be an angel and put another stick on the fire. And when I come back call me Clare. Mrs. Clayton sounds so formal and cold."

Squeak put a small log onto the fire and pushed it into place. Without meaning to she had pulled several boners, but if Mrs. Clayton—Clare—felt friendly enough for first names they apparently didn't matter. She spread out her hands in front of the blaze and decided that as soon as Clare came back she would ask her about going on the stage.

Clare Clayton was gone for at least ten minutes and when she came back her small chiseled face looked so obviously angry that Squeak didn't dare say a word. Instead she stood perfectly still while Clare Clayton walked over to the fireplace, gave the new log an exasperated poke, and then lifted up her hands with an odd, expressive gesture of despair. "Men are fools!" she said. "Idiots. That was Mark Rollins, the fat baldish man who went to church with me last night, calling from New York because he's suddenly possessed with the idea that those old books are priceless!"

"But—but maybe he's right!" Squeak burst out. "And if they are I wish you'd take them. My half, anyway. Dad said you had every legal right to them."

"The darling!" Clare Clayton said, and for an instant she looked Sunny's age. "But Mark's just an old fraud who couldn't tell a paper-backed thriller from an incunabula. What he really wanted was to go on with an argument we got into last night and when I wouldn't bite he brought up the subject of the daughter of a friend of his who thinks she wants to go on the stage and suggested that I help her. The books, which are definitely yours, were only an excuse."

"And the girl?" Squeak said, shivering. "You—you don't think she'd be any good?"

"I think she's a cheap, simpering little sponger!" Clare Clayton's voice sounded hard and ruthless. "Like this!" she said, and began pantomiming. Instantly a young, twittering fool appeared with uncomfortable clarity in front of Squeak's eyes. "So there you are," Clare said, and put down the little vase of flowers she had used as a prop. "She was raving about music last week, ballet the week before, and sculpture the week before that, and now she's hipped on the

48

stage, and is perfectly ready to exploit any man, woman, or child she thinks might be useful. I'd run five miles to escape any stage-struck girl and I'd gladly move to China to avoid this one."

Serena swallowed and for a long, drawn-out moment the only sound was the ticktock of the Empire clock on the mantel. "Can I go look at the books?" she blurted out finally. "After all, that's what I came for."

Clare Clayton put back her head and laughed. "Live forever, duckie!" she said. "The world could use a few more honest people."

"I'm sorry. I didn't mean to be rude," Squeak muttered, but Clare Clayton, who was already leading the way into the back hall, only laughed again and went on talking.

"If you only knew what a joy it is to meet someone who says what he or she really means," she said. "I'm probably getting jumpy because of Mark's protégée and another man who bothered me earlier today, but for one ghastly moment I thought you came to call because you were stage-struck too!"

Squeak stumbled and instantly Clare Clayton was beside her. "Oh, my dear," she said. "Are you all right? Did you turn your ankle? Wherever in the world is that wretched light switch?"

Squeak, who knew perfectly well that it was behind them, said nothing and Clare Clayton went back for a flashlight before they went on out to the porch. "I'm all right now," Squeak said, and as the cold, damp air blew on her cheeks she knew she had had a narrow escape which had nothing to do with her ankle. "I—I—was just clumsy."

They went down the porch steps and as they started across the wet, frozen lawn Clare Clayton stopped short. "How funny," she said. "I don't remember turning on the light in the barn. Do you suppose Miss Petersen——"

The telephone rang again and with a little exclamation of disgust she turned back to the house. "You go ahead," she told Squeak. "I'll join you as soon as I can."

Squeak kept on going, glad to have more time to herself, and a moment later pushed back the barn door and stepped inside. The minute she was over the threshold she felt, rather than saw, that there was someone there ahead of her. She hesitated and at that instant a raucous voice on her right said, "Stick 'em up or I'll shoot!"

5

Clare For a fraction of a second Squeak stood rigid. "Stick 'em up! Stick 'em up!" The voice croaked beside her, but this time she saw Mrs. Frostgate's parrot moving crab fashion along the railing of a box stall. An instant later she heard a laugh and wheeled to face Cliff Hawks.

"You!" she burst out. "What are you doing here and who brought back Long John Silver? I—I thought Anna Dugan inherited him along with the canaries."

"Well, she doesn't have him now," Cliff said. "He'd just gotten himself out of his cage by the time I came in and, boy, did he swear. Better shut the door behind you or he'll get away for good."

"I wish he would!" Squeak said, but she turned to close the door just as Clare Clayton came into the barn.

"Sorry to keep you waiting," Clare began, and then she too caught sight of Cliff and the parrot. "Ye gods, is Long John down here? The Dugans brought him over this morning as a Christmas present and I didn't have the nerve to tell them he scared me stiff. How'd he get here?"

"Stick 'em up!" the parrot said, and broke into a long string of swear words.

They all laughed and Clare Clayton grimaced. "I guess that's what did it," she said. "After the Dugans left I asked Miss Petersen to keep him in the kitchen until I could get rid of him, but if he started to swear she probably brought him down here and somehow he got out of the cage."

"Blast!" the parrot said. "Stick 'em up or I'll shoot. Blast. Blast. *Blast!*"

"Dirty thing! Such language. Dirty. Filthy!" Clare said, and now her accent and each angry awkward gesture were Miss Petersen to the life. "You stay here!" She reached for the empty cage and at the same moment the parrot jabbed forward. She jumped out of the way in time, but his hard curved beak only missed her wrist by a fraction of an inch. "Oh, Lord!" she gasped, and suddenly her voice was her own and frightened. "What can I do? Leave him in here for tonight and then pay someone to take him away tomorrow?"

Squeak hesitated, torn between a desire to help and a very real fear of the parrot's curving beak and cold eyes. "I don't know——" she began as Cliff spoke.

"Sure you don't want him?" he asked. "If I get him into that cage can I have him?"

"Of course," Clare Clayton said. "But I don't see how you're going to manage. I wouldn't go near him with a ten-foot pole."

Cliff pulled his worn gloves further up on his wrists and stepped forward. The next instant there was a scuffle of wings and claws, loud swearing, and a triumphant yelp from Cliff as he shut the cage door.

"Got him," he said. "Home free!"

"Good for you!" Clare Clayton and Squeak spoke as one, but Cliff wasn't waiting for any compliments.

"Can I borrow your flashlight and leave him in the cellar where it's warm until I can get him down to the pet shop in Braintree?"

"Yes indeed." Clare handed him the light and he started up toward the house, holding the big cage in one hand and swinging the light in the other. "Bless the boy!" Clare Clayton said as he disappeared. "I don't know what we would have done without him."

Squeak nodded and now curiosity surpassed both the admiration and the quick stab of jealousy she had felt over Cliff's success. "Why do you suppose he wanted Long John?" she asked. "He's kind of old for pets."

Clare looked at her curiously. "Cliff wants to sell him because he needs money," she said quietly. "Of course I don't know him very well, but Cousin Dorothea often wrote about him and mentioned that his family was very hard up. I know the old darling was terribly distressed when the poor boy had to shift schools so often because of his father's money troubles."

Squeak swallowed uncomfortably as she thought of the number of times she and Alice had joked about Cliff's schools. Have I ever teased him about it? she wondered, and realized miserably that at the time it had seemed both so surely his own fault and so unimportant that she didn't even know. "Golly," she began, and at that moment she heard the sound of a car on the driveway and the sharp, hacking report of a backfire. She jumped at the sound and instinctively turned toward the door, but Clare Clayton was already ahead of her and running outside. Squeak followed and caught up with her just as they saw the headlights pick out the stone lions as the car turned onto the road. "How funny," Squeak said. "Do you suppose someone has just been delivering something up at the house? Geiseler's delivery truck backfires like that."

"I don't know why anyone would be delivering anything now," Clare said, and as they saw the swinging beam of the flashlight she called out to Cliff. "Did you hear that backfire? Did you see that car?"

Cliff's face looming out of the darkness was a picture of disgust. "Worst driving I've ever seen in my life! The guy must have been parked near the south end of the drive and started up when he saw the flashlight. By the time he passed me at the house I swear he was going fifty. No wonder his bus backfired."

"Was it anyone from around here?" Squeak asked.

Cliff shrugged. "Going too fast for me to see anything except that it was a man driving a big black car. Might have been a Packard. Do you suppose he could have been waiting outside to see you, Mrs. Clayton?"

Clare turned back to the barn without answering. "Come on in and look at the books," she said. "Or we'll all freeze to death." Squeak saw that she was shaking, but whether it was from nerves or chill it was impossible to tell. She led the way to what had once been the harness room. She opened the door and as Squeak saw piles upon piles of books, she forgot everything else. "But—but there's *The Wonderful Adventures of Nils* and the Du Maurier *Society Pictures*," Squeak gasped, pointing out the familiar covers. "Those used to be in the upstairs hall. And these"—she waved to a small pile of mixed books beside her—"are Mrs. Frostgate's bedside books. Her special ones. I—I thought we were just getting the two boxes of *Mr*. Frostgate's books. This looks like every book in Holly House."

"Of course," Cliff rapped out. "Haven't you read Mrs. Frostgate's letter about the treasure?"

Squeak, with her eyes on Clare Clayton, did not even hear him. "Do you really want us to have all these?" she asked. "Every single one?"

"Every single one," Clare Clayton said. "Cousin Dorothea wanted you to have them and besides you'll be helping me. The nursery school has bought the main house for the mortgages and the back taxes and they want to move in right away. That's why Miss Petersen and I moved all of the books out of the house as soon as the appraisers were through with them."

"Who were the appraisers?" Cliff demanded. "Book experts?"

Clare shook her head. "A druggist and a real-estate man. Both local and honest as the day. They put the total value at under a hundred dollars."

"I don't believe it!" Cliff said, and at that moment Squeak saw a square white envelope lying in the dust beyond one of the piles of books. She picked it up and as she saw that it was addressed to her in Mrs. Frostgate's handwriting her heart beat faster.

"It's for me!" she said. "From Mrs. Frostgate!"

"I knew it!" Cliff bounded across the room. "I told you there was a letter!"

Squeak turned instinctively as Cliff reached for the letter, and then Clare Clayton spoke. "Clifford! That is Serena's letter. Suppose you let her read it."

Cliff froze in his tracks and Squeak opened the envelope. " 'Serena, darling,' " she began, and saw the letter was dated a week before Mrs. Frostgate's death. " 'The books are for you and Cliff Hawks. You are a real reader and will, I know, find "bread, kingdoms, stars and skies that hold them all" in this queer collection which has meant so much to me. What you decide is your own "peculiar treasure" I can't foresee, but the ultimate choice is with you. If you and Cliff need help Clare or your father will of course be ready to advise you, but the final decision rests with you. God bless you, my darling child. Your devoted old friend, Dorothea Frostgate.' "

"What does she mean?" Squeak faltered. "I—I don't understand."

"I spoke to her lawyers before I moved the books and the letters down here," Clare said. "They agree with me that it simply means you are to have first choice about everything. Cliff is to have the half that you don't want."

"I'm not so sure about that!" Cliff said angrily. "In her letter to me she said I was to have half the proceeds of any sale. Mrs. Frost-gate knew——"

"She knew exactly what she was doing," Clare said quietly, but Cliff didn't pay any attention to her.

"And what's more I don't understand why Squeak's letter was moved, hidden, probably, so it was just luck her finding it at all. Last night when we came down here both letters were propped up against the books and you told me that you wanted Squeak to find hers here just the way I found mine. That it was the next-best thing to finding them in the library, where Mrs. Frostgate had left them."

"I did say that," Clare Clayton said angrily, "and I also remember that you and I left here together last night and I haven't been back to the barn since. Yet when Serena and I came down here the light was on and you were here without an invitation."

Cliff glowered. "I saw the light from the road," he said, "and I thought you and Squeak might be working on the books, so I came in to see if I could help."

"A Chesterfield!" Clare's sarcasm was biting. "Or is it Sir Walter Raleigh? And at the same time you took the opportunity to read Squeak's letter, or did you do that last night? After all, you knew Cousin Dorothea used the word 'treasure' before Serena read it."

Cliff's face turned a blotchy red, but his voice was more angry than embarrassed when he spoke. "I read it last night when you were talking to Mr. Rollins," he said. "But when I came down here this afternoon it was moved and there wasn't a soul around except that parrot. Swearing!"

Clare laughed and suddenly the atmosphere, which had been prickly with anger and suspicion, was friendly again. "But that's it," she said. "We have been making much ado about nothing, and then some. Miss Petersen came down here with the parrot and probably started cleaning—I know she was shocked at my not dusting the books before we moved them—and when she felt cold went home without knowing she'd knocked Serena's letter out of place. And I must say I don't blame her for leaving. It's freezing down here. Do come on up to the house and we'll all warm up."

"I have to go home," Squeak said, suddenly aware of the passing of time. "I ought to have started off ages ago."

"I'll go with you," Cliff said, "but first I want to know where we can sort these books. It's too cold down here and there isn't any room at Grandma's."

"We can do it at our place. In the cobbler's shed," Squeak said, then another thought struck her. "But we'll have to hurry. Dad'll want to take over the shed in a few weeks when he starts work on his boat."

"All the better," Cliff said decidedly. "And we'll move 'em tomorrow. I'm almost sure I can borrow a truck."

"Is that all right with you?" Squeak asked, and Clare Clayton nodded enthusiastically.

"Perfect. The sooner the better! And now are you sure you won't come in and warm up before you go home?"

"I'd love it but I can't," Squeak said, and Cliff muttered something that might have been "No, thank you" and might have been something entirely different.

"What got into you?" Squeak asked as soon as they were out of earshot. "Reading my letter, and then being so rude to Clare?"

"I want to get those books moved first thing tomorrow." Cliff acted as though he had not heard Squeak's question. "If I can't borrow the Smiths' truck I'm going to call up Jube Carter. I'm in a hurry to get started."

Squeak sniffed. "Because you know Mum and Dad and even Johnny will help finish off the dirty work after you've gone back to school?"

"I want to get the work finished before your father needs the shed," Cliff said. "And besides I'm not going away to school any more. I'm starting in at the high school after this vacation."

Expelled again? The words were almost on Squeak's lips before she remembered what Clare Clayton had told her. "I—I see," she said, and then plunged on, her voice loud and aggressive from embarrassment. "But I don't see why you have to be so rude to Mrs. Clayton. I keep telling you that legally she didn't have to give us a single book, and besides she's extraordinarily friendly. I've only seen her twice and she's asked me to call her Clare."

"Oh, me too," Cliff said. "But that's because she wants to feel she's our age. And giving away the books, which she's convinced aren't worth much, is a wonderful way of making a good impression on her new neighbors. I don't think the glamorous Clare does much without thinking about her audience. Besides she's probably taken out the valuable books already."

Squeak stopped short, oblivious of a passing car that splattered them with mud. "Of all the rotten, nasty, suspicious ideas," she fumed, but Cliff only shrugged and went on walking and she had to hurry to catch up with him. "Clare doesn't even want people to know she's been on the stage," she went on. "Why, I promised her on my honor, just this afternoon, not to mention it to anyone."

"O.K., then, you did," Cliff said. "But let me tell you that yesterday that bald boy friend of hers, Mr. Rollins, kept urging her to keep this, that, and the other thing. Why, he even wanted her to go over all the clippings and junk Mrs. Frostgate always stuffed into anything she was reading."

"I don't see how that affects Clare's generosity," Squeak said, but Cliff was too wound up to listen to her.

"And I tell you this afternoon when I saw the light in the barn there was someone there ahead of me and I'll bet my shirt it wasn't

Miss Petersen. I don't know, but I'd be willing to guess that it was the man who was parked outside in that big car that backfired. Remember, Clare Clayton was annoyed at his being there, but she wasn't in the least surprised."

Squeak started to argue and explain what Clare had said about Mark Rollins and book collecting, but by that time she was so near home that she could see Grandpa Lawrence's car parked under the yard light and realized that she was really late for Christmas dinner. "Jeepers!" she burst out, and began to run. "Am I late!"

Cliff ran with her and they didn't stop until they were just outside the living room. "Be seeing you," he said shortly, and as he turned to go Squeak realized for the first time that he had walked a mile and a half out of his way to see her home.

"Golly, I bet you're late too," she said. "You probably should have gone straight home."

"For what?" Cliff asked, and as the house light outlined his shock of wet, bedraggled hair and torn jacket collar he suddenly reminded Squeak of a homeless dog. "Granny doesn't expect me unless she sees me."

"Even on Christmas?" Squeak faltered.

"Especially on Christmas!" Cliff answered, and before Squeak could say another word he headed back toward the road, whistling as he walked. She turned after him and now as she faced the living room she could see the family sitting around the fireplace and hear the strains of "Rudolph the Red-nosed Reindeer" coming from Dad's accordion. "Cliff," she called out. "Cliff Hawks. Come back and have Christmas dinner with us."

There was no answer from the road, but an instant later the front door opened and Mother's voice called out, "Squeak, darling, is that you? Where were you? We've all been so worried."

"I'm fine. I'm swell," Squeak said as she went in, and now a wave of affection and family feeling engulfed her like the warmth of the front hall. "I was just shouting after Cliff Hawks. He walked all the way home with me from Holly House and he hasn't anyplace to go where people really want him on Christmas night."

"Is he coming to us?" Mrs. Bruce instinctively turned to the dining room. "Of course you were right to ask him, but I wish I'd known about it a little earlier."

"He's not coming," Serena said, and flew upstairs to change her clothes. "I'll be down in two shakes."

She really hurried and remembered to put on her apricot taffeta dress because it was Grandpa's favorite color and he always noticed everything anybody wore. "Merry Christmas, Serena," he called out as she came downstairs again, and she knew that even in the instant it took her to cross the room he had taken in every detail of her appearance down to the nails which she hadn't had time to clean. 'You're looking very fit, my dear."

"I'm fine, Grandpa. How are you?" Squeak began, but at that moment Johnny half ran and half slid across the room, ending up with a bump against Grandpa Lawrence's knees.

"Squeak's going to be an actress, Gramp. She told us all so this morning and you ought to hear her voice when she talks actressy."

Grandpa and the rest of the family laughed and even Squeak managed to grin. "Oh, that was just a passing fancy, a joke, really," she said, and found she could turn her back on her morning self as though that Serena had never existed. "I'm not in the least stage-struck." She saw Alice's eyebrows lift and plunged on. "But we have an actress living in the village now, Grandpa. Clare Clayton. She inherited Mrs. Frostgate's house. Did you ever see her act?"

"Dinner's ready," Mrs. Bruce called, but as the others started into the dining room Dr. Lawrence continued to look down at Serena. "Clare Clayton?" he said. "I saw Basil Clayton many times,

of course. Poor chap was killed at the end of the war. Is this ᵥ.
any relation?"

"Wife. Widow, rather," Serena said, and Dr. Lawrence nodded.

"Clare Post!" he said. "Of course, now I remember. Your grandmother and I saw her in *Old Silver, Toward Desire, Valiant,* and
half a dozen other things. She's small and slight and has a truly
charming voice."

"That's the one!" Serena said, and as Grandpa held out Mother's
chair she slid into the one next to him before Johnny, who was
bringing in the soup, could claim it. "Tell me more. Was Clare
Clayton, Clare Post, really good?"

Grandpa shrugged and little amused lines on either side of his
fine old eyes deepened. "I suppose that's a matter of what generation you belong to," he said. "Personally I don't think she could
hold a candle to some of the women who were on the stage when I
left college. Still, I know she was considered to be one of the coming
stars during the late thirties and early forties and she made a really
big splash in her last play. I wish I could remember why she left
the stage just after Clayton was killed."

"Probably she was too broken-hearted to go on without him,"
Sunny said. "The poor thing."

"Maybe she wanted to go out to Hollywood," Alice put in. "But
I can't remember ever seeing her in a movie."

"No, it wasn't for either of those reasons," Grandpa said. "She
left when *Valiant,* her last play, was still going strong and it seems
to me there was some scandal about it at the time, but for the life
of me I can't remember what it was."

"Gramps, how thrilling!" Alice said.

"Poor soul, how horrible," Sunny murmured, and Mr. Bruce
nodded.

"You're right at that," he said, and began carving the turkey.

61

"People who depend on good publicity for success are really in trouble when anything goes wrong."

Only Squeak said nothing. The family voices, even the spicy smell of beet soup, faded from her consciousness. Her whole heart and mind were concentrated on a picture of herself in a new and shining role as the defender and protector of Clare Clayton's reputation.

6

"Clothed Her for Her Bridals Like the Sun"   Squeak didn't learn anything more about Clare Clayton from Grandpa Lawrence that evening, but the question of why Clare had left the stage continued to haunt her. Hours later, when she went upstairs to bed, she was still struggling to find an answer. Why, when mimicking seemed as much a part of Clare as her manicured fingers, and she obviously loved compliments about her voice, did she resent any mention of the stage?

Squeak couldn't think of a clue, so after she was in bed she reached out for *The Idylls of the King* to try and get her mind away from the puzzle which was beginning to be as tormenting as an itch. She hadn't been thrilled with the few short poems by Tennyson she had had to read at school, but the word "Idyll" was enticing and she began with *Geraint and Enid*.

Ten minutes later Squeak was completely absorbed. Enid, the good and beautiful, had been forced to give up everything she held most dear simply because her husband had misjudged her. Squeak read on and on and it came to her that Enid's story was also the story of Othello's Desdemona, which she had studied at school, and more clearly still of Clare Clayton. Of course that was the answer! Basil Clayton, the actor whom even Grandfather had called great, had suspected his wife unjustly, and because of his sudden death his widow, even in her own eyes, was never cleared.

It was long after midnight when Squeak finally finished the poem and turned out the light. Enid's life had a happy ending, Desdemona's tragic, and so in a way Clare's seemed tragic. But at least now her story was complete and plausible in Squeak's mind, and not the teasing puzzle it had been a few hours earlier. Squeak rolled over in bed and a few minutes later fell asleep only to dream of a knight at arms who also wore a torn jacket and had a gruff, boyish voice like Cliff and was accusing Squeak, herself, of infidelity.

The next morning when she woke up the house was heavy with silence. She blinked at the brilliant, reflected light on the ceiling and knew even before she looked out of the window that there must have been a heavy snowfall during the night and that the sun was shining.

By the time she was dressed and started downstairs for breakfast she saw that there was even more snow than she had thought and no sign of the town snowplow. She had just finished eating when Mother came downstairs from making Johnny's bed. "Oh, good morning, darling," she said. "I'm so glad you're up. Mrs. Hilsen can't get here because of the snow, the girls have gone off shopping, and as I have to work on the title to the Varick place I'll need you to keep an eye on Johnny. He's outside now with his new Playbowl sled."

Squeak nodded, wondering how Mum could look so enthusiastic over any job as dull as her part-time profession of title searching. "Sure, I'll watch him," she began. "If you really want——"

"Good. Splendid!" Mrs. Bruce dashed off a grocery list as she spoke. "And by the way, Miss Petersen telephoned from Holly House. They can't get the snowplow, so you'll have to put off collecting books. Just how we're going to manage sorting a lot of dirty, dusty books with the wedding coming I can't imagine."

"They're not dusty, dirty books," Squeak said hotly. "They're Mrs. Frostgate's treasures and Dad said we could go over them in the cobbler's shed."

"I'm glad you're getting them," Mrs. Bruce said, and as she gave Squeak's shoulder a light, loving little tap any sting that might have come from her quick words was gone. "But remember, love, you and Cliff will really have to hurry because Dad needs the shed to work on his boat next month."

"Oh, that'll be easy," Squeak said, and a few minutes later she put on her ski clothes and went out to find Johnny. He had just dragged his round metal-tray sled to the top of the little hill behind the house when he saw Squeak. "Hi!" he shouted. "Put on your skis and pack down the snow for me. It's so fluffy the Playbowl sled won't move without packing."

Squeak hesitated, her eyes on the cobbler's shed. There was a good chance a truck would be able to get through by afternoon and if she dug a path now and lit the little oil stove the place would be ready for Cliff and herself to start sorting. "Golly, I don't know," she began, but now Johnny was beside her.

"Ah, come on," he pleaded. "The girls have gone and Mum's so busy she's bristly. I—I've just been counting on you."

The last sentence did it and Squeak went back to the house and put on her skis. As she slid down the little hill and felt the new snow underneath her she was delighted she had given in. Now that she had decided that Clare's tragedy stemmed from her dead husband, neither the books nor Holly House itself was likely to reveal any secrets, and she was in no rush to return to them.

She did a neat kick turn when she reached Johnny, and, careful to keep her skis close together, pushed hard with her poles and slid down the hill. "That's it. That's it." Johnny jumped up and down as he shouted. "Now do that a lot of times and I'll really go zooming!"

Squeak grinned at his excitement, but she did as he asked. When she had been down the same trail several times she climbed to the top and watched Johnny start sliding off on his Playbowl. "It works!" he yelled. "It's nifty." At that moment his metal tray hit a bump, careened crazily, and an instant later he rolled off into a snowdrift. He picked himself up, snow-covered and laughing. "The start was fun," he said. "But I wish Alice was here to do the packing. She skis better than you do."

Squeak had just thought of going over to the hill behind the shed where there was a longer and better run, but now she stiffened as though someone had offered her a dare. "I can do it!" she said. "You get out of the way. I'm going to shift my weight halfway down and that'll fix it."

The first time worked perfectly. She brought her feet together at just the right moment, threw her weight onto her heels, and slid down the rest of the way, leaving an evenly packed trail behind her. "I'll do it once more," she called out. "And then you see if it isn't perfect."

She moved off again and this time she wished that Mother, Sunny, especially Clare Clayton were watching her. It's easy, really. Her mind framed the words as she slid forward. Mrs. Hilsen says skiing's simply a matter of beginning early enough. She started to shift her weight, but now her mind was on an imaginary audience and not on her skis. Her left foot overshot her right and she tumbled chin-first into the snow.

"Did you hurt yourself?" a man's voice shouted.

Squeak stood up, unhurt but feeling like a fool, and saw that Jube Carter stood at the top of the hill while the sleigh and team driven by his friend Tom Connaught were a few yards behind him.

"No. I'm all right," Squeak said, and started up the hill while Johnny dropped his Playbowl sled and rushed forward.

"Take me for a ride, Jube!" he called out. "Please. Please. I've never been in a horse sled and if I don't go now I'll bust."

Jube grinned down at him. "O.K., Johnny," he said. As Squeak came closer he went on. "Cliff Hawks got us into this. Telephoned at an ungodly hour this morning and said the town sander had broken down and would we help him move some books from the old Frostgate place. I suppose you know where they're to go?"

"Golly, yes." Squeak pointed out the shed, which looked as untouched and snowbound as an igloo. "I haven't done anything about shoveling a path or heating it."

Jube waved her into the sleigh. "Don't need a path with this rig and you can heat it later. Tom and I don't want to spend all day at it, though."

Squeak unfastened her ski bindings while Johnny still clung to Jube. "Can I go, Jube? Can I?"

"Sure thing," Jube said, and lifted him into the back seat, motioned Squeak to join him, and climbed up in front himself and took back the reins from his friend. "Oh, by the way, you know Tom, don't you?" he said. "He's going to be one of Charlie's ushers."

Squeak, who had seen him at church last night, nodded, smiling. Johnny got out an excited "Hi," Tom Connaught said, "How do you do?" in a deep Southern drawl, and amid a sudden jingle of sleigh bells they started off.

They jingled across the field, and onto the driveway. As they turned onto the road Johnny bounced up and down with joy.

"Boy, we're traveling!" he said. "Feels faster than a car, faster than a plane. Kind of magic."

Squeak squeezed his small mitten-covered hand. "It feels fast because we're so low to the ground," she said, but she knew that was only part of the answer. The quick regular thud of the horses' hoofs, the jingle of the bells, and the cold wind in their faces as they slid along all added up to something that was as good as magic if not better. She began humming under her breath and just then Tom Connaught turned in the back seat. "You all warm enough?" he asked. "We never thought to bring along a robe."

"We're fine," Squeak said, and then, on a sudden wave of liking for this sandy-haired, gray-eyed Southerner, added, "But thanks for asking."

Tom Connaught grinned and as the horses made the turn between the stone lions faced quickly forward so as not to be thrown out of his seat. Jube stopped the sleigh by the barn and Squeak saw that Cliff had spread some burlap sacks in the snow by the doorway and was already piling armloads of books on top of them. "Where's Clare, Mrs. Clayton?" Squeak asked. "Does she know you're loading?"

"Don't ask me," Cliff said, and went on working. "All I know is I'm to get every book out of here by noon."

"But we can't. We mustn't." Squeak jumped out of the sleigh. "Not without asking. It wouldn't be polite."

Cliff's big mouth turned down at the corners. "Emily Post for teen-agers," he cracked. "As far as I'm concerned Mrs. C. signed off last night."

Squeak looked up the long driveway toward the big mansard-roofed house. She was not sure what to do next, when unexpectedly Tom Connaught came to her rescue. "Suppose you and I take the little old sleigh up to the house and ask the lady," he drawled, and in that instant Squeak knew that the man in her "Idyll" had a Southern accent. "Jube and Cliff can load the books onto these burlaps, and if Miss Clayton says yes we'll load them into the sleigh in no time at all."

"And if she says no we'll have had some nice bracing exercise," Jube said sarcastically, but Cliff was already back in the barn after more books and nobody else listened to him. Johnny flung himself back into the rear seat and Squeak climbed up in front next to Tom Connaught.

"Thanks a lot," she said. "I'd have hated to move the books without asking."

Tom Connaught smiled down at her and although, with his red ears and horn-rimmed glasses, he looked no more like the man in her "Idyll" than Cliff Hawks, she knew there was something grown up and serious about him that was intriguing. "Good idea," he drawled. "And I want a chance to drive so everyone's pleased."

"I want to drive too," Johnny piped up behind them. "Right now!"

"Not a chance, little fella." The last word with its long, drawn-out final syllable was kind but very firm, and Johnny subsided. "He's just like my youngest brother," Tom went on, and now Squeak had the feeling they were definitely allies. "I reckon small fry are the same all over."

She had just time to learn that he had two younger brothers and no sisters and that his real name was Thomas Beauregard Connaught, when they reached the wide, old-fashioned veranda of Holly House. "What a house," Tom Connaught said, looking up at the wooden filigrees and ornaments. "Decorated within an inch of its life."

"Carpenter's Gothic," Squeak said, and Tom laughed so hard that she jumped down from the sled feeling decidedly witty.

She rang the bell, but Miss Petersen must have heard the sleigh, because the door opened almost instantly. "Vell, Sqveak?" Miss Petersen looked at the snow that had come in with Squeak's boots with unmitigated displeasure. "Now vat?"

"May I speak to Mrs. Clayton, please? We want to ask her about moving the books in the sleigh."

"She sleeps," Miss Petersen said. "So I telephone, when I have much work to do, to tell your mother we cannot get the snowplow and now——"

At that moment there was a rustling sound upstairs, and Clare Clayton called down over the balustrade. "Serena, is that you in that perfectly marvelous sleigh? Do come up and tell me about it."

Miss Petersen sniffed, with her eyes on Squeak's footprints, but now Squeak was unaware of her disapproval. "Cliff borrowed the sleigh from Jube Carter," she called out as she started up the broad staircase. "And he and Jube and Tom Connaught are ready to move the books in it now if that's all right with you?"

"It's wonderful," Clare said. She turned, leading the way to her bedroom, and the soft fold of her peach-colored velvet robe fanned out behind her in a graceful train.

Beautiful! Squeak thought of Enid, ". . . clothed for her bridal like the sun," and the rags Geraint had forced upon her, and felt more sure than ever that Basil Clayton had been equally cruel to his wife.

"Oh, I'm so glad you came," Clare went on, and as she took off a pretty high-heeled bedroom slipper Squeak's mind moved on to her own worn scuffies and the serviceable flannel wrapper Mum had insisted on. Clare noticed her look and her straight nose wrinkled in self-disgust. "Isn't it awful, flapping around in these at this time of day? Still, I can dress like lightning, so do go tell those boys I'll be down to help in no time flat."

"I wasn't thinking of that," Squeak said. "I was thinking how perfectly ghastly my scuffies and wrapper are compared to yours."

Clare laughed and for the second time in five minutes Squeak felt clever and appreciated. She hurried downstairs and into the sleigh and as Tom drove off she told him all about Clare's leaving the theater and of how she was sure the story was a modern, unsolved version of Enid and Geraint.

"Do you, by Jove?" Tom said, and his look of approval was as clear as a pat on the back. "That's mighty interesting. And I must say you're the first girl I've met up No'th that has ever read old Tennyson."

They had reached the barn by this time, where Cliff stood in the doorway with his arms loaded with books. "Well?" he asked, and when no one paid any attention to him he went on more aggressively. "She said O.K., didn't she?"

"Oh yes, of course." Squeak nodded vaguely and went right on talking to Tom Connaught. "Clare's really a marvelous actress. My grandfather saw her often and he says she was a great loss to the stage. *Valiant* was her last play."

"I wish I'd seen——" Tom began when Cliff bumped into him on his way to the sleigh.

"Talking about La Clayton?" Cliff asked, and put down his armload with a bang. "Well, what do you know? I thought her being on the stage was something Squeak had sworn not to mention, or was that simply a solemn oath good for Christmas Day only?"

7

The King's Mirror For an instant Squeak was stumped. Then in a flash she realized that only the truth would save her and, turning her back on Cliff, smiled up at Tom Connaught. "Wasn't it awful of me?" she said. "I did promise, you know, and then forgot all about it!"

Tom Connaught grinned back at her. "Not too serious, I reckon. And besides now we're all forewarned not to mention it when we meet."

"It's nice of you to look at it that way," Squeak said, and gave Cliff a crushing look. "I do hope you're right."

A few minutes later Clare Clayton came down in well-cut ski clothes and after the boys had been introduced they all piled books into the sleigh. They worked for about ten minutes, and then Jube called a halt. "That's enough for one load," he said. "The team can't pull any more."

Cliff stopped carrying long enough to inspect the load and Squeak saw that he looked tired and that in spite of the cold wind his face was wet with sweat. "O.K., Jube," he said. "You drive down with Tom to help you unload."

"And me!" Johnny catapulted forward and scrambled up on the front seat next to Jube. "I like horse sledding better than anything."

Squeak said nothing, but for one instant she wished she were

Johnny's age, when you could say what you wanted without worrying about what other people might think of it. At that moment Jube beckoned to her. "You'd better come along to show us where they go," he said, and without waiting for a second invitation she climbed up beside Johnny. She had just seated herself when she heard Clare Clayton laugh and turned to see that Tom Connaught had draped himself horizontally over the load of books with his thin legs bent against the front seat.

"Can you hang on there?" Jube asked, and Tom called back: "Sure thing! I feel like a wounded Roman riding on a litter!"

Jube let out the horses just as Cliff started to put one of the burlap bags between Tom Connaught's snowy feet and the books. As the sleigh moved forward Cliff gave a quick jump and, standing on the runner, held on with one hand while he stuffed the burlap in place with the other. The sleigh swerved with his weight and Jube shouted: "Get off, you dope! Do you want to get killed?"

Squeak held her breath with fear, but Cliff dropped lightly to the ground and as she turned to look at him he hurried back to the barn as though nothing whatever had happened.

"The crazy fool," Jube swore under his breath. "Does he think it's worth getting killed to save a few old books?"

"He's awfully touchy about them," Squeak said. "Last night he acted as though Clare Clayton was trying to gyp him out of a fortune, and Mum and Dad—everybody—knows they're not worth too much."

"Cliff's in a tough spot," Jube said, and it was clear he had already forgotten his anger of a moment ago. "My old man heard that Cliff's father was paying so much alimony to his second wife that there wasn't enough to send Cliff back to Yardley. I'm glad he's in this with you so he'll get a break."

Squeak said nothing as her mind rushed on to sudden, new

pictures of herself making over a fortune to Cliff with just one casually scribbled check. It's nothing, nothing at all. As usual there was a soundless word track to Squeak's imaginings. And I'm quite sure this is what darling Mrs. Frostgate intended. The fact that Squeak didn't own a checking account and that there was a very slim chance of their realizing anything like a fortune from the books didn't slow her up in the least. Her mind moved on so happily that she was actually surprised when Jube turned in at the family's driveway and Johnny shouted, "Mum. *Mum!* Come out and look at the horse sled!"

Mrs. Bruce came out to admire the horses, and Johnny scuttled into the house for some lump sugar. When the horses were fed and patted Jube drove over to the cobbler's shed.

Tom Connaught disentangled himself from the books and groaned. "That was no bed of roses," he said. "I sure feel dictionaries and concordances frozen to my ribs."

"You'll live." Jube kicked and scraped the snow away from the doorway as he spoke. "But now get going. Johnny and I'll go and pick up the last load while you help Squeak to arrange this stuff."

They carried in the books and a few moments later Jube drove off. Squeak shut the door and the cobbler's shed seemed even colder and damper than the out-of-doors. She turned toward the oil space heater, and reached out hesitantly for a box of matches. It always made her jump when the blue flames suddenly spurted upward, but this time she didn't have to worry. Tom Connaught took the matches out of her hand and lit the stove himself. "You're frozen, honey chile," he said kindly. "Better stand close and warm up for a bit."

Squeak spread out her hands in front of the quick flame and suddenly she wished that it was Tom Connaught and not Cliff who inherited the other half of the books. The only saving grace was

74

that now she understood Cliff's situation and felt sorry for him. She turned to toast her back and went on with the pleasant daydream of herself as Cliff's Lady Bountiful, his redeeming spirit, which she had begun in the sleigh. She was so engrossed that when Tom's deep voice sounded behind her she jumped. "Anthony Hope!" he said, and reached toward a pile of books on the floor. "So your lady did leave you something besides concordances."

Squeak said nothing, glad that he hadn't seen her jump, and he went on enthusiastically. "Six, eight, nine of them and except for the *Prisoner of Zenda,* which was made into a movie, they're practically impossible to get even in big libraries."

"Mrs. Frostgate had wonderful taste," Squeak said, promising herself to read one of the Hope books at the earliest possible moment.

"She sho' did!" Tom Connaught spoke without taking his eyes from the book he had picked up. "Did you ever read this—*Tristram of Blent?*"

Squeak, who had never even heard the name before, avoided a direct answer. *"The King's Mirror* is my favorite," she said, and inwardly argued that since she did like that title better than any of the others that lay on the floor in front of her she was not lying. "Much."

"Is it, now?" Tom looked impressed. "Anthony Hope liked it better than anything else he wrote, but very few people read it nowadays."

"Mrs. Frostgate was always suggesting fascinating books," Squeak said, and now that she had avoided a direct answer felt wonderfully sure of herself. "Piles of things that no one else reads."

Just then they heard the sound of sleigh bells and a moment later Cliff burst into the shed looking stocky, businesslike, and not in the least like the pathetically grateful creature Squeak had just

75

been imagining. "Oh, for crying out loud," he said. "Do you mean to say you two have just stood here jabbering without even moving these off the floor?"

"We've been discussing literature," Tom said. "We're both fans of *The King's Mirror*. Ever read it, young Hawks?"

Cliff, who had been ferreting around in the far corner of the shed, turned quickly. "No," he said. "And call me Cliff, or Hawks, or just you, but cut out this young Hawks stuff. What do you think I am, Johnny Bruce's age?"

"Sorry," Tom Connaught said good-naturedly, and then as he looked back at the piles of books gestured despairingly. "It's all very well for you to scold us for not clearing these books, but where shall we put them? What do you all plan to do for shelves?"

"Make 'em," Cliff said, and lugged out some bricks Mr. Bruce had ordered for an out-of-door fireplace. "If we use these and those clean boards over there we'll be all right. Give us a hand, will you, Jube?"

They set up six rough shelves in a matter of minutes and Tom nodded at them approvingly. "Very ingenious, these Yankees," he said. "And just to show you my heart's in the right place I'll put away *Tristram of Blent,* which I should dearly like to own." He reached out toward the books by Anthony Hope, when to Squeak's amazement Cliff stopped him. "Jeepers," he burst out. "Are these what you were talking about?"

"That's right," Squeak said. "And Cliff, you really ought to read them right away. Tom and I——"

"Not a chance!" Cliff scooped up the books as he spoke. "They aren't ours in the first place. It seems they belong to Clare Clayton and she wants 'em back pronto. She knew Mrs. Frostgate hadn't read them, and sent them to her last summer, but the old lady died before they got here."

Tom Connaught coughed and Squeak felt dizzy with embarrassment. "I think there must be some mistake," she faltered, and Cliff nodded as he went on working.

"You said it. Miss Petersen took the books down to the barn with the others and when La Clayton asked her about them and it turned out Miss P. was in the wrong, boy, did she get huffy! Wow!"

Squeak couldn't say another word. She began stacking wildly to hide her confusion and a little while later the sleigh was unloaded. Jube and Tom climbed into the front seat with Johnny in back, eager for the last little ride to the house. They had just started off when Cliff hurried after them. "Leave those Hope books at Mrs. Clayton's, will you?" he asked. "It isn't out of your way."

"Sure thing," Jube said. "And don't forget, if you find any hundred-dollar bills tucked away you're splitting fifty-fifty with me!"

Cliff nodded good-naturedly. "Sure thing. And thanks for helping."

Jube lifted his reins and as they drove off Tom Connaught turned in his seat and called out to Squeak, "Good-by, honey chile. I'd start in on *Tristram* if I were you. Leave *The King's Mirror* until you're older."

For a long, drawn-out moment Squeak gaped fishily. Finally she turned slowly on leaden feet, hoping against hope that Cliff didn't know how her bluff had been called. She needn't have worried. Cliff was already back inside the shed and as she followed him she saw that he had pulled a pad and pencil out of his pocket. "Jeepers, there's a lot to do," he said. "But first of all we'll have to check and recheck just how many books we've got, and then buy a really good padlock for this shed."

Squeak was so surprised that she completely forgot her own embarrassment. "Are you crazy?" she said. "Clare Clayton said the books had been appraised for under a hundred dollars and Mum and Dad said we'd be lucky to get fifty. Appraisers always overvalue things."

"*If* they know what they're doing. But you can't tell me a druggist and a real-estate man are book experts. And now will you start counting over there?"

Squeak was tired and after all the nervous flutter of the last few minutes suddenly cross. "I suppose you really believe Jube was serious when he made that crack about hundred-dollar bills. You probably think that was what Mrs. Frostgate meant by treasure."

Cliff jerked at something in his trouser pocket. Squeak saw it was an envelope addressed in Mrs. Frostgate's handwriting and guessed that it was the letter she had written to Cliff. Before she could say anything he had pushed the letter back into his pocket and, wheeling, looked her straight in the eye. "Will you please cut that out?" he said. "Even if you don't need money I do. No matter what Mrs. Clayton, the appraisers, or even your folks say about these books somebody wants them. Badly. So badly they made a point of sneaking into the Holly House barn to go over them when they thought they weren't being seen."

Squeak sniffed. "I thought we cleared that up yesterday," she said. "Miss Petersen was in there when she left John Silver and she turned on the light and moved some of the books."

"But the whole point is that isn't true!" Cliff said, and there was no questioning the ring of sincerity in his voice. "I asked her early this morning when I first went to Holly House. She said she hadn't moved a single book or turned on the light, but she thought she knew who had."

"Who?" Squeak said. "It couldn't have been Clare. I tell you I was with her myself."

"It wasn't any woman. It was a tall dark man, and I'd be willing to bet it was the same one we heard drive off. Miss Petersen saw him after she got back to the house when he turned on the light."

"But then why didn't she tell Clare, if she thought there was a prowler or a sneak thief going into the barn?"

"Because he wasn't. Or at least not in that sense. Miss Petersen has eyes like a hawk and she's ready to swear it was the same tall, stooped guy who'd been having sherry with Clare Clayton before lunch. With theater people crazy hours, crazy actions! You can expect anything."

Cliff's last sentence was a good imitation of Miss Petersen's bitter speech, but Squeak didn't notice it. She was no longer thinking of Holly House, but of the tall, stooped man who had tried to speak to Clare on Christmas Eve. "I wonder . . ." she began, and told Cliff exactly what had happened. "Clare really looked icy, but when she reached the car that fat man Mr. Rollins was furious at her. Do you suppose the man who tried to speak to her then could have been the same person?"

"Perhaps," Cliff said. "And in a way it all fits in if you think back to what happened. You and I were simply surprised—startled—when that car drove off last night. But as far as I could see Clare Clayton seemed angry or frightened and in an awful hurry to look at the books. Then when she saw they looked more or less all right and thought of Miss Petersen and the parrot she was obviously relieved. And that's when she really put on the heat to have us move the books as soon as possible. Do you remember?"

"Yes," Squeak said. "Did Miss Petersen say what the man looked like? More than just tall and dark and stooped?"

Cliff made a face. "You know how she is. She's so busy telling you how much she disapproves of someone she can't give you an idea of even what that person looks like."

"I know," said Squeak, who was still thinking about Christmas Eve. "Do you suppose that tall man had something to do with the

79

theater? Perhaps with Clare's last play. I had an idea that maybe Basil Clayton falsely accused her of being in love with someone else and if this were the man she probably really would hate him."

"I don't know and I don't care," Cliff said. "The whole point is, and please, please, Squeak, you have to understand that it matters, is that someone wanted very badly to look at these books. And that means that a few of them anyway, perhaps the ones we'd least expect, are valuable. Squeak, you've got to help. After all, this is for both of us."

"I will help," Squeak said, and suddenly in the face of Cliff's passionate sincerity she felt ashamed of herself. "And listen, Cliff, I really acted like a fool this morning. Tried to bluff Tom Connaught into thinking I'd read all the Anthony Hope books and I haven't even tried one."

The excitement which had lighted Cliff's ruddy, freckled face faded and he looked as expressionless and nearly as homely as a toad. I'm a fool, Squeak thought; he can use that against me any time he likes. Why didn't I keep quiet? But Cliff only looked at her for a moment and went on with his work. "I'd have done the same thing," he said. "And how!"

Squeak stared and now surprise and relief and the lovely clean feeling of having confessed left her breathless. "Tom Connaught's really very nice," she said finally. "I guess it's just because he's so much older and Southern that sometimes he seems—well, a little patronizing."

Cliff dismissed all interest in Tom Connaught's character with a shrug. For several minutes he went on working in silence while Squeak wondered if he was ever, under any circumstances, really interested in talking about people. Finally, when he had put away the two boxes of books which belonged to the long-dead Mr. Frostgate, he turned to Squeak and his face was eager and alert again. "I read about some books like these last night," he said. "Found in an old shack down on Long Island that was going to be torn down. A collector who happened to be visiting nearby looked over them before they were taken to be pulped and there was one book by a man called Junius that sold for four thousand five hundred dollars, and the rest were worthless. I'm not saying it's likely, but it is possible, Squeak, that there's something like that here."

"I suppose it is," Squeak said, and for the first time she shared a little of his excitement. "Golly, we ought to get Dad or Mrs. Tappen up at the library to help us find out which ones might be valuable."

Cliff didn't answer, but went on piling books, and then in a few moments he began to sing to himself. " 'Love learns by laughing first to speak, then slyly gains cares passing great.' "

For a moment Squeak only stared at him, surprised at the power and clarity of his voice. Cliff was short and wiry and young looking for eighteen. His gruff speaking voice was boyish, but when he sang his voice was completely a man's, and oddly stirring. He noticed her look and stopped singing. "Remember that song? It was a great favorite of Mrs. Frostgate's."

She shook her head and he rustled among the books until he found a bulging scrapbook. "It's in here," he said. "Mrs. Frostgate copied it out for me from this book last Christmas vacation."

He found the place where the words and music of the old English lyric had been pasted into the book, and pushed it toward Squeak. "You better keep it," he said. "The scrapbook, I mean. She'd have wanted you to have it."

"But how about you?" Squeak said, and added more slowly, "Don't you want it for the sentimental value? I know you were terribly fond of Mrs. Frostgate too. Don't you want it as a keepsake?"

Cliff hesitated, then as he looked around the littered room he laughed. "No," he said. "But if we want any keepsakes we'll find plenty of 'em right here. I swear Mrs. Frostgate kept everything except her clothes tucked into her books and she never remembered to take anything out."

"You're right," Squeak said, and as she glanced around at the books from which papers, ribbons, and dried flower stalks protruded like stubble in a cornfield she began to laugh too. "Golly, she was fun," she said finally. "Do you suppose we'll ever stop missing her?"

"No," Cliff said, and pushing his pencil in back of his ear, he turned to Squeak. "But now let's get to work."

8

Cliff A few minutes later they settled down to counting. Cliff worked on the books they had put on the improvised shelves while Squeak concentrated on the piles that were still on the floor. Ten, twenty, thirty-five, forty. *The sets, even the broken ones, are easy,* Squeak thought, and edged around the Stevenson to a top-heavy pile of miscellaneous books which Jube Carter had dropped near the wall. "Two hundred and five, two hundred and seven, two hundred and nine." Cliff droned the numbers out loud like a Mexican schoolboy while Squeak went on counting to herself.

She lifted up a worn calfbound copy of Milton's poems, a Greek New Testament, and intrigued by titles she didn't remember having seen at Holly House, forgot to count. There were the works of Josephus, whoever he was, in crumbling green leather, a cheap edition of Arthur Conan Doyle's *Adventures of Sherlock Holmes,* and below that a worn prayer book bulky with pressed flowers and other keepsakes.

Squeak looked at the flyleaf and saw the name "Dorothy Agnew" in a copper-plate hand and below that "from her devoted Papa at the time of her confirmation, April second, 1888." She riffled through the pages and the book opened at the "Marriage Service," where the thickest flower, a once-white rose, had been pressed between the pages. There was a card attached to the rose and Squeak read: "From my sister Mabel's wedding bouquet, June fifth, 1889." There was no other name of groom or family, but directly below the first line the words "Moving to Indiana," and then a quotation from Wordsworth's *Lucy,* "And oh the difference to me."

But that's how I feel about Sunny's leaving home! Squeak thought, and now Cliff's counting meant less to her than the buzzing of a bee. That's just how I feel!

"Listen, are you counting or reading?" Cliff turned suddenly and Squeak looked up at him through misty eyes.

"Cliff, look! Mrs. Frostgate's prayer book. The one she had as a girl. And this is from her sister Mabel's wedding bouquet. A pure white rose."

Cliff's snort of disgust was worthy of Miss Petersen. "Looks like a dirty yellow mess to me," he said. "Look at how it stained the pages of the book before it finally dried."

"You—you brute," Squeak said, and reached after him as he took the book, but he ducked too quickly for her and turned back to the flyleaf.

"Mrs. Frostgate's name wasn't Dorothy Agnew but Dorothea Adams," he said. "She told me that herself ages ago. This probably belonged to some cousin or maybe even an old friend who shuffled off ahead of her. You're wasting your tears!"

"I'm not even near crying!" Squeak said furiously. "I just have some reverence, some decent feeling for the past."

Cliff grinned. "How about a feeling for numbers?" he said. "There are four hundred and three books over here. How many have you counted?"

Squeak sat down on the floor without answering and for a moment she thought she would be safe starting at fifty. Surely that was what the bound sets had amounted to. Just then Cliff spoke. "I won't count out loud this time," he said. "That probably helped to drive whatever you'd come to out of your head."

Squeak stared at his leather-jacketed back, wondering if he had second sight, and biting her lip, began to count, conscientiously starting from the very first book. She finished counting and wrote down the number one hundred and twelve on a slip of paper. "Do I have to count a second time?" she asked.

"Of course," Cliff answered without looking up. "Definitely."

Squeak groaned and had just settled down to recounting when they heard the sound of a car down at the house and a few minutes later Alice came into the shed. "Hi," she said. "Mum wants to know if Cliff will stay for lunch?"

"If you're sure it's all right," Cliff said. "Grandma would have a cat fit over a last-minute guest."

"Mum's used to it," Alice said, and paused at the doorway. "Do you want me to telephone your grandmother and tell her you won't be home?"

"Oh, she doesn't expect me," Cliff said. "I always scrounge a sandwich or something like that on my own at lunchtime."

"Good, then it's all set," Squeak began, but now Cliff interrupted her, hurrying after Alice.

"Look, Alice. Wait a sec. Do you suppose you could help us up here after lunch? We need someone to get us started right with a good, efficient system."

A burning stab of jealousy shot through Squeak, but she forced herself to keep still as Alice answered. "Yes, I suppose so. I was planning to drive over to Centreville, but the roads haven't been sanded yet and I don't want to take the car out again in this snow."

"Good. Super!" Cliff said, and shutting the door after Alice, turned to Squeak. "Golly, that was nice of her. It's going to be a big help."

Squeak's self-control dropped off like a coat. "I don't get it!" she stormed. "Mrs. Frostgate left these books to us and not to Alice. I won't have her butting in and bossing and—and ruining everything just because she's older than I am."

"Age hasn't a thing to do with it," Cliff said. "You didn't object to Mrs. Clayton or Jube or Tom Connaught's helping, did you? And you were the one who suggested we ask your father and Mrs. Tappen about prices."

"That's different. Entirely different. Alice is very bright and efficient, but she's terribly bossy. She'll make us do everything her way!"

"Just let her try," Cliff said calmly, and added: "But I do think it's important not to tell Alice or Mrs. Clayton or even your parents about the man we think was in the barn."

"Why—why ever not?" Squeak had already planned out a fine dramatic version of that episode to tell the family at supper. Now she was so surprised she even forgot to resent his asking Alice to help. "You certainly don't think my family are going to want the books because somebody else does. I don't see the point."

"It's hard to explain." Cliff's hand moved down to the pocket where he kept Mrs. Frostgate's letter and his voice sounded as though he were struggling to think out loud. "But it's tied up with our responsibility to Mrs. Frostgate. Something queer happened about those books before they were turned over to us. But from now on we're responsible for anything that happens to them. If we can't handle that we won't be doing what the old lady wanted and expected."

"I'm not sure . . ." Squeak began, but Cliff went on speaking.

"And what's even more to the point, if your mother gets the idea there's anything queer or fishy going on she's sure to move us out of this shed so fast we won't know what hit us."

"Well, maybe," Squeak said, and then another thought struck her. "I wish you'd show me your letter from Mrs. Frostgate. After all, you read mine."

"Not now," Cliff said coolly and as he looked at her unblinkingly Squeak felt she might as well argue with a stone wall.

"But that isn't fair!" Squeak protested. "Don't you mind that both Clare Clayton and I will know you haven't been fair?"

"Not in the least," Cliff said, and as he pulled down his pencil from behind his ear and began adding up numbers Squeak realized that he really was totally unconcerned and not simply bluffing.

They worked until the clatter of the cowbell outside the kitchen window told them lunch was ready. "I've counted my books twice," Squeak said as they started down to the house. "And I get two hundred and eight. If I have to count again I'll scream."

"Mine came to five hundred and three," Cliff said. "That's seven hundred and eleven books. Even if there isn't anything like the Junius I bet Alice will think they're worth more than fifty bucks."

Squeak snorted. "Right now I'm so hungry and tired and dirty I don't care. Golly, old books are filthy!"

Nothing more was said about Alice's helping until just after they had finished lunch, when they heard the sanding machine go by on the road outside of the dining-room window. Johnny ran out to watch it and Cliff turned to Alice. "I guess that's the end of your helping us today," he said gloomily. "You won't have any trouble driving now."

Alice was already taking her jacket out of the hall closet. "Don't be a dope," she said. "I told you I'd help you and I will."

"You mean it?" Cliff's voice sounded actually startled as he followed her outside. "That's terrific!"

Squeak went into the library to put on her ski boots and Sunny settled down on the window seat with her knitting. "Poor Cliff," she said as he and Alice passed by outside on their way to the shed. "It must be ghastly to live with a grandmother who doesn't really want you and be so used to broken promises you're surprised when one is kept."

"Grim," Squeak said, and suddenly realized that she no longer resented Alice's helping and that the idea of playing Cliff's Lady Bountiful herself was absurd. Cliff had been fun and maddening by turns during their long morning together, but he was so completely independent that the idea of anyone's patronizing him was plain silly.

She stood up to pull on her jacket just as Johnny ran in from the kitchen. "Squeak! Lookit! Your name in the paper. Yours and Cliff's."

Sunny and Squeak looked at the Centreville paper he held out to them and there under "Stapleton News, Eliza Haggin, correspondent," they saw a heading: "Local Young People Share Late Resident's Libarary," and then in smaller type, "Miss Serena Bruce of Valley District and Clifford Hawks of Stapleton Centre are the recipients of a large and varied collection of books from the estate of the late Mrs. Charles Frostgate. The collection, amounting to a total of nearly eight hundred volumes, consists of poetry and prose, fiction and nonfiction amassed by the former owner of Holly House during her lifetime. There are also a number of ancient classics and religious books formerly the property of Charles Frostgate, who, before his death in 1932, was for many years a vestryman of St. Paul's Episcopal Church."

"Why, Squeak, how perfectly fascinating," Sunny said. "How do you suppose Miss Haggin heard about it?"

"Haven't an inkling," Squeak said, and turned to Johnny. "Has Mum seen the paper? Can I take it up to Cliff?"

"Mum's seen it," Johnny said. "But you tell Cliff I found that thing about you two, reading all by myself. Promise?"

"I promise," Squeak said. A moment later she ran up the hill and burst into the shed. "Cliff. Alice. Look at what Johnny found all by himself. Can you tie it?"

"Why, it's priceless," Alice said when she had read the item. "If they'd only mentioned this shed and the fact that you are going to sell a lot of the books it'd be a super ad."

"It's terrific!" Cliff said, and as Squeak looked at his happy, excited face she could guess that he was already making plans for the sale of the books. "And it doesn't make a bit of difference not mentioning this shed. Buyers are sure to try here or at Grandma's and she'll send 'em on down here. We'll call it the Cobbler's Shed Bookstall and people'll think every book here is worth millions!"

He read on, and as he turned to the next page let out a loud crow of pure triumph. "I told you so!" he said, and held the paper out so both of the girls could see the caption: " 'Famous Actress Moves To Stapleton.' Clare may kick when we mention the theater, but she doesn't shy away from publicity. Miss Haggin's got a whole long column about her and a picture!"

The two girls read the column over his shoulder, and then Alice spoke. "Mrs. Clayton may not have known a thing about it! Eliza Haggin could have picked this up in any newspaper morgue."

"That's true," Cliff admitted. "Still——"

"Of course it's true," Squeak said hotly. "After all, we didn't know Miss Haggin was going to put anything in about the books. We didn't have anything to do with that."

"Not directly." Cliff wore the smile of one who has the last word and knows it. "But indirectly I did although I didn't know it was going to work out like this."

"How? What do you mean?"

"Well, you see, when I went home on Christmas Eve after the first time Clare Clayton showed me the books, old Mrs. Chatterpuss Apsley was having tea with Grandma. They both asked me so many questions I thought I'd blow my top, but as long as Mrs. Apsley handed on the facts to Miss Haggin I guess being polite paid off!"

9

Choices   Squeak could have gone on discussing every angle of the two newspaper stories for some time, but Alice was all business. She walked around the shed glancing at the books and from the rear she looked as erect and slim as a young Amazon reviewing troops. Squeak watched her for a moment, sighed, and reached for a faded green gift book she had last seen in the drawing room at Holly House. This afternoon was going to be all work and no play if Alice had anything to do with it. Just then Alice finished her inspection of the shelves and took up a stand in front of the stove. "I think you first ought to decide which books you want to keep for yourselves and move those out of here," she began. "After that I'd put the whole sets and the brand-new novels and the mysteries, all of which you're sure to be able to sell, together. Then start a sort of question pile of the really old books that may be valuable or absolutely worthless. Mrs. Tappen may be able to help you find out the value of those up at the library and if she can't Grandpa Lawrence will."

"Grandpa Lawrence?" Squeak dropped her book and stared at Alice. "Grandpa? But he doesn't read anything like as much as Dad."

"I doubt if he reads anything except the newspapers and medical journals, but he knows a lot of collectors. Selling rare books is a cutthroat business and hasn't got anything to do with a nice cozy taste for reading. You ought to hear Professor Packer in the Fine Arts Department at college. He'd sell his soul for more incunabula."

Squeak opened her mouth to argue, but Cliff was ahead of her. "Sounds like sense to me," he said. "Would you make another pile of the really junky stuff and try and sell it for old paper?"

"Yes," Alice said, "but I'd go over it very carefully first. I think the place you're most likely to find something, though, is in the middle-aged novels. The ones published since about 1910 which might quite likely be first editions." She paused as though looking around for a good example, and then waved at a small pile of books which Squeak remembered had always stood between the elephant book ends in the middle of Mrs. Frostgate's round library table. "Even that junk might be worth something if they're modern firsts."

Squeak read the familiar titles to herself. The *Enchanted April* by Elizabeth. *Pomfret Towers* by Angela Thirkell. *The Casting Away of Mrs. Lecks and Mrs. Aleshine* and *Rudder Grange* by Frank Stockton. *Three Men in a Boat* by Jerome K. Jerome. "But those aren't rubbish," she burst out. "They're what Mrs. Frostgate called her cheerful lot!"

Alice and Cliff both laughed, but the sound was friendly and not mocking and Squeak went on. "I guess I'm being dopey," she said, "but I can't think about books and especially not Mrs. Frostgate's as though they were eggs or—or bricks or something that was just meant to sell. Books are stories, people, and the things that happen to them." She moved uneasily around the shed as she spoke. A moment later she picked up a small string-tied parcel of exceptionally battered books that she remembered seeing on the mahogany table near Mrs. Frostgate's bed. "Look at these, for instance. They're—they're as much a part of Mrs. Frostgate as her cane or her rings or something."

Alice read aloud over Squeak's shoulder. "*The Meditations of St. Augustine, Daily Strength for Daily Needs, Lyra Poetica,* and four German books. What do you bet she kept the book she really was reading on top of that lot?"

"She did," Squeak said, torn betwen loyalty and truth. "Usually a mystery story or something funny."

"Then you ought to get rid of them," Alice said decidedly. "You can't start being sentimental now or you'll never get out of the shed by the time Dad's going to need it."

"Yes—but . . ." Squeak floundered, when unexpectedly Cliff came to her rescue. He took the books out of her hand and pushed them under the tarpaulin with which they had covered the workbench.

"Out of sight out of mind," he said, and gave Squeak a quick, reassuring nod that said more plainly than words, "This is something for the two of us to settle."

"I think you're foolish," Alice said, but now as Cliff turned toward her his face was as bland as an altar boy's.

"Your idea of our taking out the books we want first makes sense," he said. "Do you suppose we could borrow your family's car and drive up to the library for advice while Squeak takes her pick?"

"Oh, I suppose so," Alice said, and Squeak looked at Cliff curiously. "How about you? When are you going to chose yours?"

"I did that yesterday." Cliff looked puckishly pleased with himself as he picked up worn copies of Gray's *Genera* in two volumes, and Peterson's *A Field Guide to the Birds.* "Here they are."

"Is that all?" Squeak asked. "Why, I'm going to take oodles."

"That's up to you." Cliff pushed the pencil behind his ear at a rakish angle as he spoke. "But don't forget we'll have to work out the price of the books you decide to keep."

Squeak started up angrily, but relaxed as she realized that Cliff's rude-sounding remark was an instinctive as his habit of pushing the pencil behind his ear. Alice was not amused. "Squeak's not in the least likely to try and cheat you," she said. "And what you said just now had all the earmarks of a very dirty dig." Squeak laughed out loud. She was touched by Alice's quick defense, but at the same time amused that her brisk and efficient elder sister had misunderstood something which she herself had grasped.

"I simply meant that Squeak and I ought to come to an agreement about the prices of the books we are going to keep." Cliff ignored both Squeak's laugh and Alice's irritation. "And as a matter of fact I think the Gray I took is probably worth any number of the books Squeak is likely to choose. They had a copy like this one at Yardley and the school librarian told me once it was worth thirty-five smackers. A really old one would probably be worth a lot more."

As usual Alice kindled to any purely practical problem. "Well, if that's how you feel about it why doesn't Squeak pick out around thirty books right now? Then when you come back if her choice is all right with you she can move them out today and you'll both start even."

"That'd be fine." Squeak spoke with her eyes on the *Whiteoaks of Jalna,* which she had been wanting to read since Thanksgiving. "How about you, Cliff?"

"Great." Cliff held open the door with mock ceremony. "But now, Alice, let's roll. You women waste too much time talking."

They went off and Squeak turned back to the shelves. By the end of a half hour she had nearly fifty books laid aside and her head was beginning to ache. She stopped for a minute to look down at the books she had chosen, and began to put a few back in the places where she had found them. After all, she didn't have any extra shelf room in her bedroom and she certainly didn't want to cheat Cliff. She put back two biographies and a book of essays, and

94

then on an impulse reached out for the prayer book that had belonged to Dorothy Agnew. The book couldn't be worth much of anything, but even if it had been she knew she would have kept it in place of a dozen other books rather than see it thrown out as trash.

She put it away, and walked over to the far corner of the shed and sat down to go over some of the piles on the floor. She was just blowing the dust off the top book when she felt the draft from the door and turned as Clare Clayton walked in. "Hello," she said, and scrambled to her feet. "How nice to see you. I wasn't expecting anyone but Cliff and Alice."

Mrs. Clayton laughed nervously. "I wasn't expecting anyone at all. When you came up like a genie out of that corner I jumped a foot. I suppose you're going over the books."

"Picking out the ones I want to keep," Squeak said, "and the more I look around the more books there seem to be that I don't know anything about and the harder it is to make up my mind."

Clare Clayton walked past the temporary shelves with the same look of concentration that Alice had worn a little while earlier. "I've done something silly," she said, and swooped down on a green clothbound book near where Cliff had left his choices. "I really intended to keep this and I suppose it was mixed up with Cousin Dorothea's books like the Anthony Hope lot that nice Carter boy returned. I hope you don't mind if I take it?"

"Of course not," Squeak said. "I only wish you'd take more. Isn't there anything else you'd like?"

Clare Clayton shook her head. "Not a thing, thanks. But I don't think Cliff Hawks is going to approve of your being so generous. I had a time this morning convincing him I wasn't actually stealing."

"I know," Squeak said, and told what Cliff had just said about the prices of the books she picked out. "Alice was furious, but the funny thing is I don't think he has any idea he's being rude or suspicious. It's as though he'd been knocked around so much that he wears chips on both shoulders as automatically as he wears socks."

Clare Clayton laughed. "Good girl," she said. "I see what Cousin Dorothea meant about your flair for understanding."

Instantly Squeak's mind filled with rosy visions in which this newly recognized talent made her even kinder than Sunny and more just than Alice. Out loud all she said was, "I get intrigued by what makes people tick."

"That's the basis for all human understanding," Clare Clayton said. "Interest fed by observation and enthusiasm. It accounts for many of the great novelists and all the village gossips."

Squeak's face fell and Clare Clayton reached over and touched her shoulder with manicured fingers. "You don't have to worry," she said. "The fact that a talent can be used or abused doesn't make it less important. Only infinitely more challenging."

She turned toward the door, and when she saw the newspaper on a nearby shelf she stopped short. "What's this? Do you mind if I look at it?"

"Of course not," Squeak said, but by the time she had spoken the three words Clare Clayton was reading intently. "Johnny found that little squib about these books, and then Cliff saw that article about you."

Clare Clayton didn't look up and Squeak went on nervously, "I hope you don't mind its being there. We didn't have anything to do with it. Both Mum and Dad hate personal publicity, but they never mind anything being in the Centreville *Star* because of Miss Haggin."

Still Clare said nothing and as Squeak rattled on her voice sounded gushing and squeaky even in her own ears. "Miss Haggin's a really good reporter, you know. She had a wonderful job on the New York *Herald Tribune* and had to give it up when her mother got paralyzed and she had to come home to take care of her. She's been writing the Stapleton columns ever since."

Finally Clare put the paper down. "I expect your friend Cliff was delighted with the publicity on the books," she said dryly. "But don't forget I warned you against being too generous. He definitely won't like that."

A moment later she was gone and Squeak turned back to the books, which seemed dustier and less glamorous than ever. She added one or two more volumes to her chosen pile, but her mind wasn't on her work and a few moments later she absent-mindedly took them away again. I'm an idiot, she thought. Clare read that article right under my nose and I didn't even find out whether she minded its being there. What a washout. Then as the door opened and Cliff stamped in alone Squeak turned toward him eagerly, glad of any excuse to leave the books. "Where's Alice?" she asked. "And what did you find out from Mrs. Tappen?"

"Alice went over to the Carters'," Cliff said, and slammed down the armful of books he had taken along as a sample. "And our trip was a dud. Mrs. Tappen said we'd be lucky if we got fifty cents for the bunch I took up. She said she'd order a guide to first editions for us, but otherwise the library was a complete flop."

Squeak stood up and found that her back ached from moving books. "What do you mean, a flop? It's a marvelous library and Mrs. Tappen's an exceptional librarian. Dad's always saying Stapleton's fantastically lucky."

"We didn't go for a nice cozy read or even to do homework," Cliff said crossly. "We wanted dope on book prices, first editions, rarities, and we didn't find out a thing."

"Well, we'll just have to ask Grandpa Lawrence, then. He's

coming up over Sunny's wedding. And here are the books I want to keep."

Cliff took one subject at a time. "You write to your grandfather tonight," he said. "And ask him if there are any books about books, especially their value, that he could bring along. Most of the stuff probably isn't worth a nickel. Mrs. Tappen said the library was forever getting donations of stacks of books from people's attics and that almost all of it was pure junk. Only worth pulping."

"Well, we're not going to pulp the ones I picked out to keep," Squeak said. "If they're all right with you why don't you get Johnny's sled and we can take them down to the house right now."

"Good idea." Cliff only glanced at the books and reached for his cap. "Do you want to write down the titles and authors while I get the sled?"

Squeak didn't want to do anything at the moment but go down to the house and soak in a hot bath laced with plenty of Sunny's bath salts, but she managed to nod good-naturedly. "O.K.," she said, "and I bet I'll get it all done before you find the sled."

Cliff went out and Squeak started writing down names. Once or twice she paused, not certain whether she wanted to keep the book she had picked up or not, and then went on scribbling. She was almost finished when Cliff burst through the door so suddenly that she jumped. "You scared me to death," she said. "Just the way I scared Clare Clayton a little while ago."

Cliff dropped the sled on the cement floor. "Was she down here? This afternoon? Whatever for?"

"Oh, just to pick up a book," Squeak said, and wrote down the last title and author.

"What book?" Cliff demanded. "Why did she want it? And why did you let her have it without asking me?"

"Oh, don't be like that," Squeak said, and now she was too tired

and cross even to think about being understanding. "This was hers,
I guess. Like the Anthony Hopes. Just an old book of plays by somebody Mantle. It was over near your Gray's *Genera*."

Cliff crossed the shed in two strides. "I remember that book," he
said, and pounded down his fist so the loose boards rattled. "It was
right here."

"So what?" Squeak said, and began piling her choices onto the
little sled. "I tell you it was a book of plays and she knew neither
of us would be interested. You don't read plays, do you? Except
when you have to at school?"

"That hasn't anything to do with it. What I want to know is why
couldn't she have taken it this morning or, better still, day before
yesterday when she and I first went over the books? Why did she
have to wait and come sneaking down here when she knew I wasn't
around?"

Squeak looked at him incredulously. "Are you crazy?" she demanded. "Or just so suspicious it amounts to the same thing?"

"Neither," Cliff said furiously. "I just happen to know that book
was in the second load and she must have seen it this morning,
because after the Anthony Hope mix-up we went through the lot
with a fine-tooth comb to see if there was anything else that belonged to her. And what's more she knew I wasn't going to be here
this afternoon, because Alice and I met her as we were going in the
library and told her what we were planning to do. I bet my shirt
she came down here when she knew I was away, because she was
absolutely certain she could talk you into anything. You get so intrigued hashing over what people say and think and feel that you
don't even notice what they do! And it's hard enough to tell when
Clare's acting and when she means something, anyway."

A sharp, sarcastic answer dried unspoken on Squeak's tongue.
Cliff was infuriating, but there was enough truth in his last sen-

tence to make her unsure of herself. She stood still for an instant, groping for the right, the telling words in which to prove to him that as far as she was concerned Clare Clayton was above suspicion, but the words didn't come and she ended up by loading her books onto the sled in silence.

Neither of them spoke until they had pulled the books down to the house. They found Sunny alone in the living room, writing at Mrs. Bruce's desk. "You're the hardest-working pair I know," she said, and nodded toward their loaded arms. "That sort of work makes going over wedding lists look like a rest cure."

Squeak grinned, feeling easier and more confident as she always did when Sunny was around. "This is dirtier, anyway," she began, and would have told Sunny more about the afternoon, but Cliff interrupted. "Where do you want these put? In here?"

"No, in the upstairs hall," Squeak said, and lead the way with her own armful.

Cliff carried up the last load and started for the front door when Sunny called to him. "Cliff, stop a minute. Charlie and I want to know if you'll come to our wedding. We can't ask many people to the reception, but we'd like to have you. Friday the tenth, at four."

"Thanks, sure. I guess I can make it," Cliff said, and he sounded so offhand that Squeak wanted to slap him and to scold Sunny for asking him.

She didn't say anything, but Sunny must have sensed her irritation because now she turned to her smiling. "How about you, Squeak? Isn't there someone you'd like to have invited specially for you?"

Squeak, who had wandered over to the window, turned and as she glanced at Cliff saw the perfect way to squelch him and at the same time to attest her loyalty to Clare Clayton. "Why, yes, there is," she said coolly. "Clare. You know, Mrs. Clayton. I think she'd love to come."

"Good," Sunny said, and wrote down the name. "I know Charlie would love to meet her."

Cliff grunted and left the room without looking at either Sunny or Squeak. "I'll be back to work on the books first thing tomorrow," he said as he reached the door. "And I'm bringing along a padlock!"

10

Spider Web The next morning Squeak overslept. By the time she had helped herself to breakfast in the kitchen all of the family but Sunny, who was busy sewing upstairs, had gone out, so she decided to go straight up to the shed.

She put on her out-of-doors clothes and found her back and shoulders were stiff from moving books. It's hard, dull work, she thought as she tramped over the crusty surface of the snow on her way to the shed. This afternoon I'm going skiing no matter what Cliff says!

A moment later she reached the little building and saw the padlock that Cliff had already put on the door. For an instant she was only aware that he had been there ahead of her, and then as she pulled on the doorknob realized that he had gone away again and locked her out.

She pulled and pulled again, but the padlock held and she started back to the house. The wind was sharp and blew gustily around her ears and neck. She shivered and chilliness and the cross, left-behind feeling which oversleeping always gave her merged into a near tantrum directed solely at Cliff Hawks. He had a nerve, locking her out from her family's shed and her own or at least half her own books. She went into the house and called upstairs to Sunny. "Did

Cliff Hawks leave a key here? Did he say anything about the padlock? The big dope's locked me out."

"Oh, what a shame." Sunny's voice floated down from the upstairs. "He didn't leave a thing. Poor boy, he'll feel terrible when he knows what he's done."

Squeak snorted and, stopping only long enough to pick up a heavier muffler, went outside again. She headed for the road, but when she reached it hesitated, not sure of what to do next. She wanted to reach Cliff and those keys pronto, but unless she walked the mile and a half to his grandmother's she didn't know of any way she could get into the shed. Squeak started to walk down the road, and as a car came along and stopped, she had what seemed like the first break of the morning. The car was driven by Mrs. Apsley. The old lady turned down her window and leaned out so that the sun glittered on her square-cut glasses. "Good morning, Serena. Can I give you a lift?"

"Thanks a million." Squeak climbed into the front seat. "I'm going up to the Center and now that the roads are cleared it's impossible to ski."

Mrs. Apsley let in her clutch and leaned over her wheel as though after all these years it might suddenly turn into a skittish horse and leap out from under her. "I'm going right up there," she said. "But now do tell me all about your inheritance. I hear Dorothea Frostgate left you and the Hawks boy all her books, and that that cousin of hers who was on the stage is simply furious."

Squeak had known Mrs. Apsley's reputation as a busybody all her life, but even so she was amazed at the malice in her last sentence. "But—but Mrs. Clayton's been terribly nice about the whole thing," she said. "According to both Mum and Dad, there was no legal reason for her turning the books over to Cliff and me at all. They weren't mentioned in Mrs. Frostgate's will. Just in some letters that weren't witnessed or anything."

"Oh? Indeed?" Mrs. Apsley sounded disappointed, but as they turned in to the center she brightened. "Where shall I leave you, childie? I suppose you're doing errands for Mother? I know with all the outside things she does she must count on you girls. Going to the market or did I hear she was trading with Geiseler?"

"Right here'll be fine." Squeak was suddenly inspired to be vague. "I think perhaps later on I'll go to the library."

"Then I'll take you right to the door. It won't be a mite of trouble." Mrs. Apsley's overbright, overcheerful voice set Squeak's teeth on edge. "A pleasure, I'm sure."

"Thank you very much," Squeak said as she got out. She turned away, and suddenly realizing that Mrs. Apsley was leaning forward and watching her, dashed up the library steps fuming to herself.

Mrs. Tappen, the pretty, prematurely white-haired librarian, who was Squeak's favorite person in her parents' generation, looked up smiling as she came in. "Hello, dear. You look in a hurry. Can I do anything to help you?"

"I'm looking for Cliff Hawks. I don't suppose he's been here this morning."

Mrs. Tappen shook her head. "Not since he and Alice were here yesterday. I was so sorry I couldn't do more to help them. Cliff seemed terribly disappointed."

Squeak shrugged. "Cliff's hipped on old Mrs. Frostgate's books being absolutely priceless. He even gets upset if I take time out to read a paragraph."

Mrs. Tappen laughed. "Well, you're a born reader and he's not," she said, and then turned to a tall middle-aged man whom Squeak didn't know. "Can I help you find anything?"

The man nodded and Squeak wondered where she had seen him before. "If it isn't too much trouble I'd like very much to see your Elzevirs," he said. "I found in the catalogue that you have several locked away."

"We have three." Mrs. Tappen picked up a key. "And months go by and no one even asks to see them. Now if you come with me I'll be delighted to take them out for you."

She went over to the library's treasure cabinet with the tall man following her. Squeak looked after them, and as the man reached out eagerly, even before Mrs. Tappen turned with the books in her hand, she knew where she had seen him before. Christmas Eve, in the snow. He was the man who had approached Clare Clayton with his hands out in this same gesture of eagerness, only to be instantly dismissed.

Squeak turned, and walking slowly out of the library, almost bumped into Mrs. Apsley. "Leaving so soon?" the old lady asked. "Didn't you find what you wanted? Couldn't Mrs. Tappen help you?"

"Yes. No. Thanks." Squeak answered mechanically, too absorbed in her thoughts of the tall man to notice or be annoyed by the old lady's curiosity.

Squeak went on down the library steps to the village street and turned right. She was certain that the man she had just seen was the one who had accosted Clare on Christmas Eve behind the church and it seemed more than possible that he was also the one whom Cliff had disturbed in the barn at Holly House.

I don't get it, Squeak thought. Suddenly she realized that she had walked past Cliff's grandmother's house, turned back, and rang the bell. Miss Petersen opened the door, but Squeak, who knew that she worked for old Mrs. Hawks a few mornings a week, was not surprised. "Hi," she said. "How's Mrs. Hilsen? Is her cold any better?"

"Some." Miss Petersen opened the door a few cautious inches. "But I don't think she ought to work this week. You want to see Cliff? He's out."

"Do you know where he went?" Squeak began, but at that moment they both heard Mrs. Hawks in the parlor to the right of the front door.

"Miss Petersen! The draft. Please, do you have to keep that door open so long? Who is it, anyway?"

Squeak would have backed away, but now Miss Petersen caught her by the elbow and propelled her toward the parlor. "You go tell her what you want," she whispered. "She can't blame that draft on me."

Squeak went on into the hot, overfurnished room, which she had been in once before ages ago when she and Dad had brought Cliff home from a children's party. Mrs. Hawks, dressed in black, was in her wheel chair playing an intricate form of solitaire, but she pushed it away from her as Squeak came in, and wheeled over to shake hands. "Good morning, Serena," she said, and, pointing to a red plush chair where Squeak was to sit, wheeled herself noiselessly beside it. "I suppose you're looking for Clifford? I thought he was down at your house, but of course he never tells me where he's going. Never. Grandmother's just a convenience. Perhaps if his mother had lived or his first stepmother had behaved herself it might be different. As it is, no one can say I haven't done my duty."

Squeak felt her skin crawl with embarrassment. "Cliff's swell," she blurted out, and the words sounded forced and silly in her own ears. "He probably is down at our house right now. I'll go back and look for him there."

Mrs. Hawks gave her wheel chair a half turn so that it partially blocked Squeak's way to the door. "Oh, don't go yet," she begged. "You don't know how I count on visitors for news. Tell me about your family and your older sister. She's getting married week after next, I hear. Is it going to be a big wedding?"

"No, it isn't," Squeak said, and now she felt so sorry for the old lady that she forced herself to tell her what she could about the wedding plans, the bridesmaids' dresses, and any other details she thought might interest her.

Mrs. Hawks listened intently, asked a few pertinent questions, and as Squeak rose to leave put out her hand pleadingly. "Do tell me something about the books. I never knew Dorothea Frostgate well, but I imagine she had interesting things. Cliff only tells me how many there are and what he hopes they're worth."

I can believe that, Squeak thought. She began to name the first titles that came into her mind and found that she was already thinking in terms of the categories that Alice had suggested yesterday. Trash, queries, hopefuls, middlemen, and keepies. She ended with the books she had selected for herself, and stood up before Mrs. Hawks could stop her. "I really have to go now," she said, and tried not to sound too desperate. "Mum'll be expecting me."

"Well, it has been a pleasure to see you," Mrs. Hawks said, and, apparently satisfied that Squeak was really going, wheeled herself back to the card table. "I hope you find Clifford, but I know it isn't easy. As I told his father last week I can't keep an eye on him at all times. Not at my age . . ."

The faint complaining voice followed Squeak into the hall and she slid out through the door, grateful that she wasn't expected to answer. Once outside, she took a deep breath of the clean, frosty air, and then started to walk quickly homeward.

The wind brushed her cheeks as she walked and now after Mrs. Hawks' stuffy parlor the fresh coldness was as welcome as a good wash after a walk through cobwebs. Cobwebs. Whew. The analogy was too apt for comfort. Mrs. Hawks was pathetic, pitiful, but she was also incredibly like a large black spider moving soundlessly in her wheel chair after any fly of news. Squeak grimaced, and then, leaving the village street, took the short cut down a narrow dirt road for home. Poor Cliff, she thought, and every vestige of pity that she had felt for Mrs. Hawks was submerged in her sympathy for Cliff. Poor guy, if I had to live there I'd blow up! She walked on, suddenly ashamed that yesterday, only a few minutes after Clare Clayton had complimented her on being understanding, she had been as short-tempered with Cliff as though she were still at the sandbox age fighting back some other toddler who had taken her shovel. She was within sight of home now, and as she looked up at the plain, roomy old building every angle of it seemed welcome and precious after Mrs. Hawks' hot, overfurnished house. I will do better, she promised herself. The next time I want to brain Cliff I'll remember what it must be like to live in a spider web.

She reached home just in time for lunch and learned that although Lyb Harris and another school friend had telephoned to ask her to go skiing there was no message from Cliff. The idea of skiing was more tempting than ever, but she was still so fired by her resolve of the morning that she decided against it and hurried up to the shed as soon as lunch was over.

Cliff was not there and the door was as tightly padlocked as ever. She turned on her heel, fighting down her disappointment and crossness, and was just starting toward the house when a car stopped on the road below her and a moment later Cliff came panting up the little hill. "Hi," he said, and sounded as offhand as Johnny. "I've just been over to Centerville. I guess you were locked out."

"I'm counting ten so I won't bite," Squeak said. "I came up here to work this morning and there was no way of getting in. Then I went up to the center to look for you, and no dice. And this is probably one of the few days of perfect skiing we'll get all winter. I feel gypped."

Cliff laughed and handed her an extra key, and unlocked the padlock with the other one. "Too bad," he said. "But when Ed Sutor offered to drive me over to Holly House and then down to the pet shop in Centerville I didn't dare take the time to stop down at your house with the key. I had a super-duper morning and it won't happen again."

"It better hadn't!" Squeak said, and then curiosity overcame her. "How much did you get for Long John Silver?"

"Twenty dollars," Cliff said. "And believe it or not that was only one reason why the morning was so terrific. I saw Clare Clayton after I sold him and she couldn't have been nicer. Wouldn't take a cent of the money and made me feel like a big shot for having offered it. And what's more I found out why she wanted that Mantle book and now I don't even blame her much for getting it as quietly as possible. It isn't a book of plays, it's a book about plays and her last play, *Valiant*, was right in the middle of it."

"Cliff. No. Did she show it to you?"

"Nope," Cliff said, "and since she's got a grudge against the theater and I guess especially about that play, I don't suppose she ever will. But it was on the table in the living room when I was in there waiting for her to come down. I picked it up and it opened right up to the cast of characters and a picture of Clare, because someone, probably old Mrs. Frostgate, had left a paper napkin there as a bookmark. The picture makes Clare look about half the age she is now and if you ask me that's probably what she's really touchy about. She doesn't want anything noised around about her real age. But anyway the point is I'm sure now that she isn't out to gyp us about the books or anything else."

"Good," Squeak said. "I'm glad." Then she remembered the man whom she had seen in the library that morning, and told Cliff all about him. "Do you suppose he could have been after Clare to let him go over the books first?" she ended up. "And that that's why she was so angry at him and so eager to get them moved over here?"

"Could be," Cliff said, and carefully hung up the padlock on an inside hook. "At any rate, this won't be wasted."

Squeak nodded, but her mind was much more on Clare Clayton than on locking away books. "Or, Cliff, do you suppose that man could have come in between her and her husband somehow and that's why she hates him?"

"I haven't an idea," he said, and took Squeak by the shoulders and moved her gently but firmly toward the shelves. "But now get to work on the sets. Some are broken and from what Mrs. Tappen says we'll practically have to give those away, so let's pile 'em on the floor." He pushed the pencil behind his right ear and it was clear he was through talking.

"Slave driver!" Squeak said out loud, but she knew he was making sense and a moment later she set to work herself.

By four o'clock they had finished sorting the sets and had begun on the miscellaneous novels. "Boy, I'm stiff," Squeak groaned as she kneeled down to go over a pile on the floor.

"Me too," Cliff spoke without stopping work. "And in all the wrong places." Squeak looked over at him. His face was streaked and dirty from book dust and sweat and when she realized that her own was probably just as bad she laughed out loud.

"We're a messy-looking pair," she said. "I need to go to a beauty parlor and be made over from the ground up."

Cliff grinned and broke into a song that was just going the rounds of Stapleton:

"Oh you can't go to Heaven in powder and paint
'Cause the Lord don't like you as you ain't."

Squeak grinned and put out her hand. "Help me up," she said, "and I'll struggle back to work *as is!*"

Cliff reached out and had just pulled her to her feet when there was a loud knock on the door. The sound was so sudden and unexpected that Squeak jumped. Cliff's arm went around her waist. Just then the door opened and as the tall man whom Squeak had seen at the library walked in she jerked away.

The tall man smiled down at both of them and then coughed. "Oh, I am sorry," he said. "I didn't mean to interrupt anything—er—private."

II

Fox Fur For a long embarrassing moment nobody spoke. Then Cliff stepped forward with his hands on his hips and his lean chin out. "What do you want?" he demanded. "What are you looking for?"

"Won't you—won't you come in?" Squeak's attempted courtesy sounded flat and fluttery. The man was already walking around the shed looking as much at ease as though he were glancing at the shelves in his favorite bookstore.

"I'm interested in your books," he said pleasantly. "That charming librarian up in the village said you had inherited quite a collection. Is this the lot?"

"Yes, it——" Squeak began, when Cliff interrupted. "These books are for sale," he said roughly. "For cash. When we know what they're worth."

The man glanced back at the nearest shelf and shrugged. "I'm afraid you may be in for a disappointment," he said. "From what I can see most of these books are only worth pulping. That's so often the case with books that have been left to dry rot in an attic." He waved his gloves toward the books that had always stood on the center of Mrs. Frostgate's round library table. "These, for example. Typical out-of-date, unread dead wood."

"But—they're not!" Squeak burst out. "They're not dead wood

and they certainly aren't unread. Mrs. Frostgate was especially fond of them and I—we—feel handling them is a—a sacred trust!"

The man raised his eyebrows. "Sentimental values are different, of course. And I suppose your parents or some other adults have already advised you about the cash values?"

"We're handling this ourselves," Cliff said. "And we have to be out of this shed in a very short time, so we haven't time for sightseers. Do you want to buy something or not?"

Squeak choked at Cliff's rudeness, but the tall man only laughed. "As a matter of fact I do," he said. "If you have anything I can use. Books on the theater, plays, modern poetry. Ezra Pound, T. S. Eliot—that sort of thing."

"Mrs. Frostgate thought they were gloomy, so we haven't too much," Squeak said, and then for the first time noticed that Cliff was following the man's every move as though he expected him to pick up the books and run. The man noticed it too and turned to Cliff, smiling. "I'm really not a thief, old chap," he said, "and, just to prove it, I'll give you five dollars for those four books you have tied up over there."

He nodded toward the books Cliff had taken up to the library the day before and for the second time in a short while Cliff's face grew beety. "They're not worth it," he said, and he sounded as though each word hurt. "We were told we'd be lucky if we got ten cents apiece for them."

"All the more reason for them to prove my good faith," the man said, and pulled a crisp five-dollar bill from his pocket and pushed it at Cliff just as Johnny opened the shed door and came in.

"Hi," he said, and eyed the stranger before he went on with his message. "Cliff, your grandmother wants to speak to you on the telephone and, Squeak, Mum says you're to beat it right down to the house and get snazzed up. Dad's home already and Mrs. Clayton's coming for tea."

Cliff hesitated for a moment, the five-dollar bill in his hand, and then as Johnny pulled at his sleeve he pocketed the money and moved toward the door. "I'm coming," he told Johnny, and called back over his shoulder to Squeak. "You better stay here until I get back. I won't take a sec!"

He and Johnny disappeared toward the house and the tall man picked up his books. "Suspicious young chap, your boy friend. Still, I expect it's a good characteristic."

"Cliff isn't—I mean he doesn't," Squeak floundered, but the man only laughed and motioned to her to precede him through the door.

"I'm not complaining, only complimenting," he said. "But now I really have to go myself. Perhaps I'll stop in again some time if I'm motoring through here."

Squeak nodded, too fussed and embarrassed to speak, and hurried to the right toward the house while the man went straight ahead the road, where he had left his car. Cliff isn't my boy friend, she thought angrily. How can I help it if he's rude?

She went on into the house and heard Clare Clayton's voice in the library and on her other side Cliff's voice, gruff and reluctant, speaking over the kitchen telephone. "Yes, Grandma. No, Grandma. I understand, Grandma." She poked her head around the kitchen doorway.

"He left," she called out, and tore upstairs to change her shoes and comb her hair. When she came down again Cliff was standing just inside the library door.

"I have to go," he said, and looked hungrily at the cinnamon buns Alice was bringing in from the kitchen. "Grandma wants me to pick up some stuff at the drugstore and that's a good long walk out of the way."

"I'll take you," Mr. Bruce said, and made room for Squeak between Mrs. Clayton and himself on the window seat. "I have to go up to the center to a vestry meeting at six."

"O.K." Cliff seemed to find it hard to say thank you, but his oddly expressive face looked grateful and he began to help Johnny, passing the tea food without being asked.

"How are you coming along on the books?" Clare Clayton asked. "When I saw that second sleigh load go off yesterday I was certain the Bruce family would never speak to me again. Two sleigh loads of dusty, dirty books in a household that's having a wedding soon does seem like an imposition."

Mrs. Bruce laughed as she poured out the tea. "It would have been a headache right here in the house," she said. "But the cobbler's shop is perfect as long as they can be through by the time Jack wants to start work on his boat."

"We'll manage," Cliff said, and then Johnny, who had polished off three cinnamon rolls in succession, came into the conversation.

"Who was the tall guy who was up there when I came to get you?" he asked. "His hair looked like a black and white fox."

"Our first customer," Cliff said. "He paid five dollars for four books we told him weren't worth fifty cents. The ones we took up to the library yesterday, Alice."

"Not really," Alice began, and Squeak turned impulsively to Clare Clayton.

"I think perhaps you know the man," she said. "He came up to you after church on Christmas Eve. A tall, good-looking man with black hair sprinkled with white."

Squeak thought she felt Clare Clayton's body grow tense, but when she spoke her voice only sounded amused. "I'm afraid quite a few people answer that description. Your father, for instance."

Mr. Bruce bowed elaborately and during the laughter that followed Clare Clayton moved over to ask for another cup of tea and sat down beside Sunny. Does Clare know who it is? Squeak wondered. Is it someone she hates or loves or is she afraid of him? Is he connected in her mind with her husband or the theater or what? It was impossible to tell.

Right now Clare was asking Sunny about her wedding and listening to the answers as though she didn't have another interest in the world. She's as bad as Mrs. Pike and Mrs. Rankin, Squeak thought of two of her mother's friends with engaged daughters. Then another, an uncomfortable suspicion clouded out everything else. Was Clare really so interested in how Sunny's silver was to be marked, or was she simply acting the role of mother-of-the-bride the way she had acted a stage-struck girl and a little later Miss Hulda Petersen?

A few minutes later Clare Clayton rose to leave, and when Mr. Bruce went to see her to her car both Cliff and Squeak wandered out after him. "Listen, Cliff," Squeak began when Clare was safely seated behind the driving wheel. "What do you——"

She never finished the sentence. Cliff grabbed her arm so that it hurt, and then plunged off through the snow toward the cobbler's shed. "You left the light on!" he called out. "And the door's wide open!"

Squeak followed after him, heedless of the snow that came up over the sides of her loafers. "Cliff! The door was shut. That man shut it after me. I'm—I'm positive."

"It's a—cinch—you—didn't lock it!" Cliff got out. As they reached the doorway they were both so startled by the mess in front of them that for a moment they only stood still and gaped!

Books were on the floor and the piles of sets were knocked sideways. One of the temporary shelves was halfway down. The armful of Mrs. Frostgate's "cheerful" books lay every which way and the things which had been inside the books were strewn over the floor. Squeak stared at the pathetic clutter of bookmarks, pressed flowers, clippings, and letters. "The stinker!" she got out. "He must have come back here after I went down to the house."

Cliff was already struggling to push back the bricks under the sagging shelf before more books fell. "Give me a hand on this," he ordered. "Or we'll have the whole thing down."

Squeak steadied the books while he got the bricks back into place, and then he faced her, his eyes blazing with anger. "We haven't an idea who did this, not a clue," he rapped out. "Anyone could have come up here from the road, and down at the house we wouldn't have heard a sound."

"Footprints. In the snow, Cliff. We ought to be able to find out something from that."

He raced out ahead of her and as she followed him into the cold her heart sank. The light from the shed picked up a bright crystal-line reflection on the snow, but there were so many footprints around the doorway that it was impossible to separate them. She moved on, heedless of the wind, and saw crisscross above the narrow marks of the sleigh the wide tracks of car tires. "L-look," she said, and found her teeth were chattering with the cold. "A car. What do you bet that man came back here from the road after I left?"

Cliff grunted, pushed Squeak back into the shed and slammed the door. "Get in before you freeze to death," he said. "Those tire marks don't prove a thing. Practically every car in town, in the whole country, for that matter, would make tracks like that."

"But—but Cliff, what are we going to do?" Squeak wailed. "Whoever it was may have taken anything, the most valuable thing here, and we'll never know."

"Oh yes we will," Cliff said grimly, and set to work straightening up the piles on the floor. "We counted, remember, and this morning while you were asleep and before I went to Centreville I checked and rechecked."

"I see," Squeak said humbly, and she too fell to work putting back the books on the shelves and picking up the pitiful flotsam and jetsam on the floor. They worked feverishly for twenty minutes. Then Cliff straightened up for a moment and stood staring at the shelves with his hands on his hips.

"I don't know," he said. "And I won't know until we've counted and recounted, but so help me Hannah I can't see that anything is missing."

"Thank goodness for that!" Squeak turned from the workbench, and as she faced the permanent shelves beside the doorway she started forward. "Cliff! The books we sold that man, Fox Fur. They're right there and I know, *I absolutely know* he took them with him. It must have been he—him who came back here."

Cliff reached the parcel of books ahead of her and lifted them curiously. "Are you positive?" he said. "It isn't just something you dreamed up or imagined?"

"On my absolute word of honor I'm positive," Squeak said. "I can still see him tucking them under his arm."

"I believe you," Cliff began. Just then they both heard the sound of Mr. Bruce's horn, loud and insistent from the courtyard. "I'll have to go," Cliff said. "But I'll be back here first thing in the morning. Have you got your key to the padlock?"

"Yes," Squeak said, and now, suddenly aware that Cliff had neither blamed nor scolded her for not locking the door, she rushed on, "And I'll work here this evening, Cliff. I'll get the stuff back in place, anyway, and then tomorrow when we're both here we can count."

"O.K." Cliff nodded abruptly, opened the shed door, and disappeared.

By the end of half an hour Squeak had everything in fairly good order. She was just turning to go when she saw a faded snapshot of Mrs. Frostgate's son in his World War I uniform lying directly in front of her, and realized the tall man must have dropped it out of one of the books. She picked it up and when she saw it was wet and dirty from the floor her heart pounded with anger. Of all the rotten tricks! she thought, and now she could hardly wait to tell the family about the man who had ransacked the shed. She snapped off the lights, fastened the padlock, and started toward the house. She moved quickly, but her mind, spinning and turning on the dramatic story she had to tell, outpaced her feet and her rapidly beating heart.

Mr. Bruce was not home yet, but all the rest of the family was in the library when she burst in. Mrs. Bruce noticed her wet feet first. "Really, Squeak," she began, and then when she saw Squeak's face she sprang from her chair. "Squeak, what happened? Are you hurt? You look frozen to death."

"I'm all right. But Mum, Alice, the most absolutely incredible thing happened! That man, the one we told you about, came back and rifled, ransacked, messed up every inch of the shed."

She rushed on with her story and made the tall man sound ominous and sinister from the moment he had stepped over the threshold of the shed. "It was really terrific," she ended up. "You can't believe what the shed looked like and my heart was beating so I could hardly move."

For a fraction of a second there was silence. Then three Bruces spoke at once.

"Jeepers!" "How awful." "Squeak, darling!"

"Did you lose anything?" Only Alice sounded calm and matter-of-fact. "And how did you know it was the same man back again?"

Squeak told her about the parcel of books, and added, "Of course,

I don't know what is missing. Cliff thinks we didn't lose anything, but we won't really be sure until we count tomorrow."

"I don't like it at all," Mrs. Bruce said, and as Mr. Bruce came in she hurried to meet him in the front hall. "Jack, did Cliff tell you about the perfectly horrid thing that just happened up at the shed?"

Mr. Bruce came into the room and his pleasant face looked as serene and kindly as usual. "Cliff did say something about someone poking around through the books," he said, and for the first time Squeak had an uncomfortable suspicion that she had overdramatized her story. "I gather he was annoyed and all that, but he didn't sound as though he thought anything had been stolen."

"I'm sure there wasn't!" Squeak put in. "Probably that man was just curious or something."

"I think it's extremely disagreeable," Mrs. Bruce said. "And now you'd better get ready for supper, Squeak."

Squeak went upstairs to change into dry shoes. The suspicion that she had said too much grew and spread until her whole body felt as cold and clammy as her feet. She took her time in changing in the hope that when she went downstairs Mum would be thinking about something else.

It was no use. The family were all at the dinner table by the time she went down again, but they were still talking about the tall stranger's visit to the shed.

"This must not happen again," Mum said as Squeak sat down. "I like to help out Eliza Haggin, but I can't help feeling her article is the cause of it and I simply cannot have complete strangers poking around this place. Why, they might come down here and take the silver or Sunny's wedding presents or anything."

"Oh, I'm sure that wouldn't happen!" Squeak wished with all her heart that she had painted a less sinister portrait of the tall stranger. "The man was awfully well dressed and sort of prosperous."

"That's all very pretty," Mother said, and it was clear that she was talking to Father and not paying any attention to Squeak at all. "But we certainly can't have people we don't know anything about streaming onto this place. The children will simply have to get rid of the books without having people we don't know coming down to paw over everything. Don't you agree with me, Jack?"

"Yes, I do," Mr. Bruce said, and the very calmness of his voice told Squeak the whole matter was settled. "From now on I think you and Cliff will have to understand that the shed is a place to sort the books but not a secondhand junk shop."

12

Skiing That night it took Squeak a long time to go to sleep. She tried to conjure up a new chapter in "The Idyll," but neither that nor any other pleasant idea took root in her mind. No matter which way she twisted and turned she couldn't forget what Mum and Dad had said about selling books from the shed. Cliff's wonderful plans were ruined, it was all her fault, and worst of all she was going to have to tell him so.

The next morning the alarm clock woke her at half-past seven. She got up and began dressing immediately, and now that the time was so near when she would have to tell Cliff what had happened she felt more depressed than ever.

It was only after she had gone up to the shed and found that she was ahead of Cliff that she began to feel a little more cheerful. Surely if he found her hard at work by half-past eight he couldn't be too angry with her.

The little building was icy cold and as Squeak nervously lit the stove she remembered Tom Connaught lighting it for her. For an instant she wished all over again that Tom Connaught had inherited the other half of the books, but as she straightened up and looked around the crowded shelves Tom's image faded. Tom was polite and well read, but it was impossible to imagine his doing the back-breaking work Cliff took in his stride. Oh, if I only didn't have to tell Cliff about not selling from here, she thought. If only I'd kept my mouth shut last night! Just then she heard the crunch of footsteps in the snow outside and Cliff came into the shed.

"You're early," she said, and her heart sank further than ever as she saw he looked tired and depressed. "I—I didn't expect you for hours."

"I got a lift from the milkman," Cliff said, and held his red, chapped-looking hands toward the stove. "I knew he had this route."

"Neat idea," Squeak said, but Cliff, who usually crowed over any small triumph like a free ride, didn't say a word. He hung up his cap, stuck his pencil behind his ear, and began putting more supports under the temporary shelves without even glancing at her.

"I finished cleaning up that man, Fox Fur's, mess last night," Squeak said nervously. "And now I'm going to sort Mrs. Frostgate's cheerful books. You and Alice were absolutely right about not getting sentimental over them."

Still Cliff said nothing and the bad news Squeak had to tell him pressed inside of her like heartburn. He's in an awful mood, she thought miserably. I'd better wait. She started to sort books, but she couldn't concentrate on a single title. I just can't stand this, she decided, and, turning quickly, plunged into an exact account of what had happened when she had told her family about the stranger's visit to the shed. "It was all my fault," she finished. "I only wanted to tell a good story, but I—I guess I spoke out of turn."

For a tense moment neither of them spoke. Then Cliff burst out laughing. Squeak stared. "Cliff Hawks, do you understand what I've done?" she asked. "It isn't funny."

"Don't I know it?" Cliff said, and laughed harder than ever. "But the point is I did the same thing. Talked out of turn last night. And the funny part is that it reminds me of something that happened ages ago with Mrs. Frostgate."

Squeak's mouth opened and shut, and Cliff went on more soberly. "It's not the same thing, really," he said. "Except the way you and she both called my bluff by being honest. You see, years ago when I was a little kid and staying with Grandma there wasn't much to do. So one morning I wandered over to that orchard near Holly House and began to pick and eat some peaches. Then I saw Mrs. Frostgate and nearly died of fright. She looked at me and laughed and asked if I knew I was trespassing. I was too scared to speak, but just nodded, with peach juice dribbling all the way down to my chest. She roared with laughter and said so was she, that the orchard belonged to somebody else and that maybe we'd both better go back to Holly House and get cleaned up before we were caught. After that I never came within miles of Stapleton without going over to see her first thing."

Squeak grinned. "Sounds just like her. I got to know her when I was in third grade and began to walk home from school just so I could really see the stone lions. I thought if you said the right magic word they'd come to life and even Mum laughed, but Mrs. Frostgate didn't. But I don't understand about last night. I know you talked to Dad, but from what he said you didn't make it sound overdramatic or scary."

"It wasn't that," Cliff said. "It was after supper when I went over to Holly House to ask Clare Clayton about Fox Fur that I really put my foot in it. But the laugh is that I wouldn't have said a word about it if you hadn't been so darned honest."

Any compliment, no matter how left-handed, was rare, coming from Cliff, but this one passed Squeak unnoticed. "*You* asked Clare about Fox Fur," she gasped. "What in the world did she say?"

"Nothing!" Cliff said disgustedly. "Dressed up in a lot of ice-coated frills. And then when I pointed out you were almost sure you'd seen her talking to him after church and that I had a hunch he was around Holly House on Christmas Day she really jumped me. Said who she saw and what she said was her own business and if we were going to make a point of acting like a pair of Peeping Toms she'd go out of her way to take back all the books."

"Cliff! She didn't!"

"Oh, yes she did," Cliff said. "But she was so angry I know she didn't mean it. In fact she practically said so herself just as I left. Still, it's a cinch we're not going to find out a thing about Fox Fur from her!"

"But, Cliff, that's fascinating. I'll bet anything he was in love with her and when she turned him down he tried to come in between her and her husband. Why, it's the very essence of drama, don't you see that?"

"I don't see a thing," Cliff said briskly, and for the first time that morning he sounded like his usual self. "Except that I'm sick and tired of any and all acting this side of the movies. You said yourself that the reason why we can't sell books from here is because you practically made your mother believe Fox Fur held us up at the point of a gun."

A dozen angry answers flooded through Squeak's mind in fewer seconds, but she didn't say any of them. "I'm sorry," she said finally. "I did make it all sound pretty terrific."

Cliff only nodded, and, reaching for his pencil, turned to the shelves. "I'm going to count now," he said. "And when we're certain nothing's missing we've got to start thinking about distribution. It's going to be a real headache when you haven't a license and Grandma hasn't a car."

" 'Oh, you can't go to heaven in a limousine!' " Squeak chanted another verse of the song they had sung two days earlier and Cliff came in on the chorus: " 'Cause the Lord don't sell no gasoline!' " Then he motioned for silence as he settled back to counting. Finally he turned away from the shelves and his face looked relieved. "There isn't anything missing!" he said. "Fox Fur made a mess, but he didn't take a thing. And d'you know, I'm beginning to think we won't lose much by not being able to sell from here. The second-hand bookstores in New York are going to be our best bet anyway. The tough thing will be getting the books down there."

"Oh, that won't be too hard," Squeak said. "After Sunny's wedding Mum's sure to drive down more often and maybe she could take them down for us."

"And drive around from one secondhand bookstore to another between her shopping and stuff?" Cliff said scornfully. "It wouldn't make sense even if we could persuade her to do it."

"Oh well." Squeak refused to be discouraged. "Somebody's always driving down to New York from here and maybe Mum could arrange for us to go along and take the books by degrees. She's a whiz at fixing up things like that."

"She's a whiz, period!" Cliff said. "For my money she's got it over Madame Clayton like a tent."

Squeak was so surprised she dropped the book she was holding. "But you can't compare them," she said. "Clare Clayton is—was—a distinguished actress with a tragic, mysterious past and Mum's swell, of course, but you couldn't call her glamorous."

Cliff grimaced and it was clear he was irritated at having been tricked into discussing personalities. "I like people who come clean with you," he said. "Like your mother and old Mrs. Frostgate."

"But Clare comes cl——" Squeak said, and as she thought of yesterday afternoon, stopped in the middle of her sentence and began again. "Clare's so—so vibrant herself she brings out the best in other people. Sort of challenges you into standing on your tiptoes mentally and spiritually, if you know what I mean."

Cliff snorted. "Oh, come off it," he said, and nodded, grinning, at his own worn ski boots. "She just makes me think of the size of my feet. But let's skip it, Squeak, and get on with the books. If we work like crazy for the next half hour we ought to be able to finish up before lunch everything we can do until we get that first-edition guide. I want to go skiing this afternoon."

"That's good with me," Squeak said feelingly. "If you ask me, this is an awful tough way to spend Christmas holidays."

They did finish their work that morning and in the afternoon Squeak went out skiing with Alice and Sunny. Sunny, who was no athlete, hated the town hill and they set out for the long gentle slopes behind the cobbler's shed with Johnny, pulling his Playbowl sled, trailing behind them.

"The three big Bruces—ski like gooses!" he chanted. "The three big Bruces!"

Sunny giggled, tripped, and almost fell over the end of her own skis. "You two go ahead," she said. "I'm going to find something about the size of a molehill to practice on."

"I'll stay and keep you company and maybe make a snow man," Johnny said, so Alice and Squeak went on alone to the longest hill. Alice went down first and a moment later Squeak, feeling as though she were part of a fighter squadron peeling off into the air, swooped after her. She made the hill perfectly and as she slid to a stop at the bottom her whole body tingled with delight.

They practiced turns for the better part of an hour, and then moved on to the southerly slopes that dropped more sharply into the valley. By the time they came back to the top of the first hill a short, squat snow man was waiting to greet them, but Johnny and Sunny had already gone indoors. They went down the hill half a dozen times in rapid succession and each run was faster and more exciting than the last.

"Cliff was going over to Town Hill," Squeak said when they

rested for a moment before their last run. "Is it any better than this?"

"Not as good except for the ski tow." Alice began pushing herself forward as she spoke. "Too many people, and the snow was wearing thin even yesterday. I bet before today's over there'll be at least one real crack-up. Well, here goes!"

She moved off, crouching as she swept over the crest, and straightening up as she slid more slowly into the purpling shadows in the valley. Squeak gripped her ski poles and plunged after her. The run was faster than ever now that the sun had set, but after her hours of practice Squeak felt completely confident.

Her knees were springy and relaxed and her arms with their flashing ski poles kept her so perfectly in balance that she had no desire to drag the pole discs to slow down. She was so wrapped up in the joy of speeding, swooping, flying down the hill that it was a surprise when she reached the bottom, and found that Alice had been watching her. "You've gotten a lot better than you were last winter," Alice said. "If there's good snow on Friday, Jube and a lot of us are going over to Mohawk for the day to ski. Want to come?"

"Golly, yes!" Squeak emphasized her words with a neat quick kick turn and fairly pranced across the level space. "I've wanted to try that ski tow for ages."

"You could handle it easily," Alice said, and Squeak glowed with exercise and pleasure. She began to herringbone up the hill and now a whole new vision of herself as an expert skier, a second Andrea Lawrence, unfolded itself in her mind.

They crossed the level stretch on top of the slope in silence, but as they came within sight of the cobbler's shed Alice spoke. "How'd Cliff take the news about not selling from here?" she asked. "Did he blow up?"

"He didn't say much," Squeak said, but suddenly it dawned on

128

her that if she went to Mohawk on Friday she'd lose a whole day of work on the books. *I didn't promise him,* she told herself. *He can work if he likes. There's no reason on earth why I shouldn't go.*

She moved more slowly, so that she fell behind Alice and was all by herself as she passed the shed. The little building looked lonely and mutely reproachful in the twilight and Squeak turned her head away. *This is crazy,* she thought, but no matter which way she turned she could not bring back the lovely pictures of herself skiing superbly in Norway, or Switzerland, or Sun Valley. "Hey, Alice. Wait for me!" she called out, and struggled to forget the shed, the books, and Cliff by racing after her sister.

They left their skis on the porch and had just gone into the house when they saw Mrs. Bruce hurrying down the stairs. "My, I'm glad to see you two!" she burst out. "I was just going to send Johnny out to tell you that it was too dark to ski. There's been a dreadful accident over at Town Hill and I think it made me jumpy."

Alice walked on into the hall, but Squeak stood rooted by the front door, feeling as though something were squeezing down on her so that she couldn't breathe. "What a shame," Alice said, and took off her scarf and mittens. "Who was hurt?"

"Not Cliff!" the two words came out of Squeak's dry mouth like a protest. "Not Cliff, dead?"

For an instant Mrs. Bruce and Alice only stared at her in amazement, and then Mrs. Bruce said, "Why, of course not, honey. It wasn't a fatal accident and it wasn't anyone we know. They were two boys from Stamford, I believe, and one broke his ankle and the other dislocated his collarbone. I happened to hear about it when I stopped in at the fish market."

"Tough luck for them," Alice said, and hung up her ski jacket. "I said that hill was too crowded."

Squeak leaned over to unlace her ski boots and now waves of embarrassment and relief swept over her so that her skin prickled. "Cliff did call up, though," Mrs. Bruce went on. "It was just after I reached home and he said that first-edition book you wanted had come and that he'd be down with it first thing tomorrow morning."

"That's a relief!" Alice teased. "I'm sure Squeak would have stayed awake all night worrying about the books and Cliff if he hadn't called."

Squeak wanted to stamp her feet and swear with anger, but she knew she would burst into tears if she said a word, so she stalked upstairs and down the hall to her own room without even looking at Alice. The tears were hot in her eyes by the time she reached the bathroom, but she didn't make a sound until she had the water from both taps roaring noisily into the tub. Then she spoke out loud as though Mother and Alice and Sunny too were just waiting to be convinced. "I'm sick and tired of the books," she said. "And I just can't stand Cliff Hawks."

13

Before the Wedding   Even after Squeak had had a long leisurely
tub and put on clean clothes she felt edgy as to what Mother might
think and Alice say about her sudden outburst. By the time she
finally went downstairs again the family were all at the supper
table, but they were still talking about the accident. Mr. Bruce had
heard more details down at the railroad station and Johnny asked
him so many questions that Squeak thought the subject would
never change. Finally Alice brought up the bridesmaids' dresses
and Mother nodded as she began to serve the desert. "Oh yes, and
that reminds me that Squeak and I'll have to go over to Centreville
for her fitting tomorrow afternoon. I'm afraid we'll have to leave
right after luncheon because I'll simply have to finish the Varick
title while I'm over at the town hall."

"I'll be ready," Squeak said out loud, while inside her mind her
conscience popped up like a jack-in-the-box and began prating in
an ugly Punch-like voice that only Squeak could hear. You knew
that was coming, but you forgot to tell Cliff, the voice said. You
knew about that fitting and yet you went right ahead and accepted
to go to Mohawk for all of the day after tomorrow.

As soon as supper was over she went upstairs to write to Grandpa
Lawrence and somehow the fact that she still didn't think the letter
was necessary made her conscience easier. After all Gramps had

heard about the books at Christmas and he was coming up to stay over Sunny's wedding, so it was simply giving in to Cliff's bossiness to write ahead of time. She wrote about moving the books and the work they had done and asked for advice about collector's handbooks. She paused for a moment, and as a new idea came to her, dashed on, "If you have any old price lists or marked auction catalogues you could send on before the wedding it would be wonderful. We have to get out of the shed before February first, when Dad plans to start work on the *Esmeralda* and with school (ugh!) starting up on Wednesday we haven't too much time."

She was so pleased with the letter that she decided against setting the alarm and settled down in bed to read *Rebecca,* by Daphne du Maurier, which was one of the books she had chosen to keep. The story was so exciting that it was after midnight before she finally put out the light. She fell asleep at once, but she didn't wake up until Johnny came into her room to ask her to fix a broken shoelace and to tell her that most of the snow had melted.

Squeak yawned as she tied his shoelace together. She glanced at the clock and saw that it was half-past ten. She shooed Johnny out of her room and hurried into her clothes. Cliff would have been working for hours by the time she reached the shed, and this time if he was cross Squeak couldn't possibly blame him. She raced downstairs and had just bolted some breakfast when Alice came in from the garage. "No snow," she said disgustedly. "And Jube just called up and said the Mohawk trip was off. Apparently it's melted even faster over there than here."

"Too bad," Squeak said, but when she went outside and started up toward the shed she felt secretly relieved to see mud and tawny-colored grass where yesterday there had been snow.

Cliff was sitting on the orange crate when she reached the shed, holding a small green book in his left hand and a larger blue volume in the right. "Browsing?" Squeak cracked. "Through two books at the same time?"

Cliff didn't even turn to look at her. "You're late," he said. "But listen, Squeak; I stopped in at the library for the first-edition guide and it works like a charm. You just have to find out the publisher of any book and then this guide gives you their special symbols for a first edition. It's a pipe!"

Squeak was intrigued in spite of herself. She looked over Cliff's shoulder and saw that the blue book was Booth Tarkington's *Penrod,* published by Doubleday Page, and that the small green book was H. S. Boutell's *First Editions of Today and How to Tell Them.* "Do you see how it works?" Cliff asked. "Doubleday Page put the words 'First Edition' right underneath the copyright notice, but Harcourt, Brace & Co. put a number. The only out is we still don't know if there's any demand for the first editions we turn up."

"When I wrote Gramps I asked him for price lists and marked auction catalogues," Squeak said. "Those ought to help."

"Bright idea!" Cliff was so unexpectedly approving that Squeak decided to make the most of it. "I won't be able to work this afternoon," she said. "Bridesmaid's dress-fitting over at Centreville."

"Well, why didn't you say so yesterday when we were making plans?" Cliff sounded so schoolmasterish that Squeak was suddenly cross. "I thought I'd finally made you understand we've got to use every hour we can on these books."

"Don't be silly," Squeak said. "I still have a few other interests. In fact if the snow hadn't melted I was planning to go over to Mohawk tomorrow with Alice and Jube and a crowd."

"You slay me!" Cliff said, and laughed out loud as he reached for another book. "You really slay me."

"What's so funny?" Squeak snapped. "I don't see anything funny about Mohawk."

"There isn't," Cliff said, but he was still chuckling. "And I'd have been sore as a boil if you'd gone. It's just I think it's a howl you're telling me when otherwise I'd never have known about it. You're more like Alice and your ma and old Mrs. Frostgate than you think. None of you can help being honest."

Squeak smiled and her sudden anger disappeared even more quickly than yesterday's snow. She could have gone on talking about Mrs. Frostgate and herself for hours but as usual Cliff was all business. "You start feeding me books from the question pile," he said. "If you read the title page and I check with the guide we ought to be able to make time."

"Here's *Caravan* by John Galsworthy," Squeak said, but her mind was still on the unexpected compliment Cliff had paid her. "Maybe it's worth quite a lot."

Cliff craned his neck to look at the book she was holding and then reached out and dropped it on a pile away from the stove. "It says *third* printing," he said coldly. "Try again."

The next book was *So Big,* by Edna Ferber, and Squeak gave out a little yelp of delight when she saw the words "First Edition" under the publisher's imprint. "This one starts the 'ought to be worth something pile,'" she said, and spread down a clean piece of newspaper on the floor beside her. "I hope we get dozens."

They went through nearly thirty books without coming upon any more firsts. "Did you ever know so many editions?" Squeak said. "Every single one is a second or a third or an umpteenth edition."

"They really should be called printings or impressions," Cliff said, and read aloud the introductory note in his guidebook. "We're going to end up being real rare-book experts, you and I."

"Maybe," Squeak said, but as she reached for *Jeremy and Hamlet,* by Hugh Walpole, and turned to the title page she was

134

so completely engrossed with the work at hand that no elaborate fantasies of a future as a book collector entered her mind. "This was published by Cassell and Company in 1923 and there's no other date."

"Then it's a first edition." Cliff turned to Cassell and Company in his guide. "Add it to the good pile."

Squeak reached for *The Battle-Ground,* by Ellen Glasgow, and when it turned out to be a third impression her straight nose wrinkled with disgust. "Still, it's fun, Cliff," she said as she went over to the shelves to bring down more books. "Kind of like fishing. You always hope the next bite is going to be the big one."

The morning flew and Squeak was almost sorry when it was time to go down to lunch. Cliff had brought some sandwiches and a thermos bottle of coffee with him, and was planning to work the whole day. "I'll have gone through the lot by tomorrow morning," he promised. "You wait and see."

"Wonderful," Squeak said, but the next morning when they met at the shed and started in on the longer and more tedious job of writing down the title, author, and physical condition of every even possibly salable book she wished they were back at checking. "This is awfully dull," she said when they stopped at noon. "And how do we know this is what book buyers want to know?"

"Because I called up Schulte's, the big secondhand store in New York, last night," Cliff said. "So if you're just stalling you'd better think up a better excuse."

Squeak groaned, but that afternoon she came back to the shed immediately after lunch and stayed at work until even Cliff said that he could feel lists coming out of his ears and that they had better call it a day. They worked hard for the rest of the week. Gradually Squeak found that she was no longer thinking of the books in connection with Holly House or Mrs. Frostgate or even in terms of stories, play, and poems she might want to read, but simply as an assignment, a challenging chore that was alternately interesting and dull, but had to be finished within a given time.

Near the end of the vacation they began to reassemble the books on the shelves and in piles on the floor according to their own carefully worked out classifications. At four o'clock Cliff, who had been doing the lion's share of the heavy work, stopped long enough to walk slowly all around the shed. His hands, like Squeak's, were grimy with book dust and there was a black smudge on the side of his cheek where his hand had touched it in reaching up for his pencil, but his expression was decidedly cheerful. "Yesterday I was so fed up I'd almost have been glad to see Fox Fur," he said. "But today even though the shed looks more of a mess than ever I feel sort of hopeful."

Squeak, who felt exactly the same way, nodded and lines from *Henry V* which were favorites of her father's popped into her mind. " 'Let me speak proudly . . .' " she quoted. " 'We are but warriors for the working day; Our gayness and our gilt are all besmirch'd with rainy marching in the painful field . . . And time hath worn us into slovenry: But, by the mass, our hearts are in the trim'!"

Cliff, who was standing by the window with his back to the shed, said nothing, and Squeak wished that she had kept her quotation to herself. She struggled to think of some flip, bright crack to cover herself, when Cliff spoke without turning around. "Say that again, will you?" he said, and, wondering, she did as he asked.

He turned as she finished and she looked up at him, suddenly aching to have him say something, anything to tell her that he loved the words as she did and had understood. He didn't say a word and as he set to work tying up parcels of books his face was as withdrawn and expressionless as a house with closed shutters.

They worked in silence until it was time to leave, when Cliff began to stalk around the shed. "School starts tomorrow," he said, and sounded as though he were talking to himself. "And with Sunny's wedding so near you won't be much use. I hope I can get through on time."

"Of course *we* will!" Squeak angrily emphasized the word "we." "I've done my share of the work this week, haven't I?"

Cliff grinned and suddenly he reminded Squeak of the small, cocky Peter Pan-like Cliff who had been wished on her at children's parties years ago.

"Oh, I suppose you did what you could," he said airily. "I'm just trying to plot out the work that's still to be done. I know with Sunny's wedding coming up you'll be useless for days."

Squeak was too irritated to answer, and by the next day when she saw Cliff again she had forgotten all about it. The morning school bus was crowded and as Cliff was a senior and she was a junior she didn't have a chance to speak to him until after school hours when he got off the afternoon bus just behind her. "Hi there," she said. "How'd you like your new school?"

Cliff shrugged. "One more new school isn't a thing in my life. But now come on up to the shed. We've got at least an hour and a half before I'll have to go home."

"I'm not going," Squeak said, and stopped foursquare by the path as though she dared him to push her. "This is the week of Sunny's wedding and you can include me out."

"I told you that's the way it would be," Cliff said, but his grin was good-natured as he pulled out the notebook he used working on the books, and walked on up toward the shed alone.

Cliff left the bus with Squeak every day for the rest of the week and went straight to the shed to work until suppertime. Once Squeak went up to help him, but most of the time she was too busy helping Mum and the girls with the growing list of things to be done before the wedding. The days flew even faster than during the vacation and in no time at all it was Thursday the ninth, which was the day Charlie Reed's leave began and the night his family were giving a supper dance for the wedding party at the country club.

Cliff and Squeak walked from the bus together as usual and as she turned toward the house and he headed for the shed he called back over his shoulder. "I'm coming back to work after supper, so if you see the lights don't worry. I'll probably get here about the time you come back from the rehearsal."

"Stop in and have a Coke and something to eat before we leave for the Reeds' party," Squeak called out, and instantly a picture of herself in her new dress offering a grateful Cliff refreshments filled her mind. *You're beautiful!* the imaginary Cliff said, *Squeak, Serena, why didn't I ever realize that before?*

The real Cliff only waved at Alice, who had just come out of the front door. "Call me when you want me to come down," he said, but Squeak, who had suddenly remembered that Alice was going to drive her over to the rehearsal right after school, didn't hear him.

"I'm coming, Alice," she called out. "I won't be a second."

Several of the ushers were late for the rehearsal and by the time the Bruces reached home again it was time to dress for the party. Squeak bathed first, and took out the net dress Mum had bought at a sale the day she had tried on her bridesmaid's dress. She knew Mum had been right about its being a bargain, but now as she put on the aquamarine stole in front of the mirror she realized that it was the most becoming dress she had ever had.

A few minutes later she went downstairs singing to herself. She had learned at the rehearsal that the Reeds had engaged Bert Hurd's "Pacemakers" to play at the party, and suddenly Squeak felt as though she couldn't wait for the dancing to begin. " 'I am as corny as Kansas in August,' " Squeak sang, and kept time with her new silver slippers. " 'High as the flag on the Fourth of July.' "

"A bevy of beauties," Dad said when everybody had collected in the library. "Charlie Reed and Johnny and I are lucky fellows."

"You look sensational yourself, Jack darling," Mum said, and for once she didn't act as though she were waiting for the telephone to ring or wondering how she could finish off the errands on her list. "I wish we had more excuses for getting all dressed up."

A moment later Charlie came in to drive Sunny to the party, and then Jube Carter and Tom Connaught came for Alice. "Can Serena come with us, Mr. Bruce?" Tom asked. "I would have called you all up earlier, only I didn't like to bother you."

"Of course," Mr. Bruce said, and when he and Mrs. Bruce and Johnny went out to the family car Tom helped Squeak with her wrap.

"You see, I really have to catch up with you, honey chile," Tom drawled. "I want to know whether you've done your homework on Anthony Hope."

For an instant Squeak was tempted to bluff again, only warily this time, expertly, so she would never be found out. She turned to face him and as she did so she caught a glimpse of the lighted shed through the library window and changed her mind. "I haven't read one single line of any of them," she said, and whisked the stole over her shoulders. "The only one I'd ever heard of before was the *Prisoner of Zenda* because I saw the movie."

"Oh, my stars!" Tom Connaught roared with approving laughter. "The little Yankee isn't only bright and pretty as a picture, but honest, so help me!"

Jube and Alice had already gone out to the car and now Tom

caught Squeak's hand and hurried after them. "Come on, Serena. I feel partyish!"

"So do I!" Squeak felt herself floating on a starry cloud of lightness, gaiety, and fun. "Oh, so do I!"

"All aboard?" Jube asked, and shot out of the driveway. Behind them the door of the cobbler's shed opened and for an instant Cliff's lean, erect body was silhouetted against the light. None of the four in the car saw the light, nor did Squeak think of her invitation of a few hours earlier. School, homework, Cliff, and the cobbler's shed seemed more remote than the moon.

14

Before and After A few minutes later when Squeak and the others arrived at the country club the party was well under way. As they passed the locker rooms she heard the sound of voices and laughter ahead of her, and over and above it all the lilting strains of The Pacemakers playing "Wish You Were Here."

The Bruces did not belong to the country club and Squeak had been there only once or twice for meetings and scout rallies. She remembered that in the daytime the big main room was plain and barnlike, but now as she followed Alice over the threshold she stepped into a wonderland of crystal and silver, of cellophane icicles and crepe-paper snow men. "Mary Reed and Harriet Tucker did all the decorations," Alice said, and although her voice was approving it sounded as calm and down to earth as ever. "Sunny chose the right pair of gals for bridesmaids."

"It's a knockout," Tom Connaught said. "A regular steam-heated fairy ice palace."

Squeak nodded, too excited to speak. Just then she saw Johnny, still pink and scrubbed-looking from Mrs. Hilsen's final grooming, sliding toward her across the polished floor. "Jeepers, Squeakie, isn't it super!" he called out. "And Mary Reed and Harriet say I can have the snow men after the party. For real keeps, Squeakie!"

"Good. Wonderful!" Squeak didn't even notice the nickname

that she hated. The Pacemakers had switched into "Shopping 'Round," which was one of her favorite tunes, and now Jack Reed, Charlie's brother and best man, came across the floor at the head of what looked like a black-jacketed patrol of Reed cousins and stag friends from law school, college, and army camp.

"Alice. Squeak!" he called out. "Wait a sec. These chaps want to be introduced. Boy, do we need bridesmaids!"

From then on the evening popped with excitements like the corks which Joe Gambrell, the club waiter, pulled from bottles of chilled champagne. Music, toasts, compliments, laughter, and for the bridesmaids an apparently unlimited supply of extra men eager for dances.

At supper Squeak found herself seated between Tom Connaught and Seth Reed, a cousin who was a senior at Princeton. Both the men were good dancers, but between the four other ushers and the cousins and uncles on her own and the Reed side of the family she never had a chance to go more than halfway around the room with either of them. Even Grandpa Lawrence, looking handsomer than ever with his silver-white hair and well-cut evening clothes, waltzed with Sunny, and a moment later Johnny came over to Squeak and made his own interpretation of the Norwegian bow Mrs. Hilsen had taught him. "Come on," he said, and his round cheeks were cherry red from excitement. "I want to try dancing."

Johnny pushed Squeak halfway around the room before Tom Connaught cut in.

"I like your family," he said as they glided away from Johnny, "I can hardly wait for my Heather to meet you all."

"Heather? Who's Heather?" Squeak asked and guessed even before he answered her that he was talking about his fiancee.

"Heather Randolph is my girl," Tom said, and Squeak realized with a little tingle of self-satisfaction that she was not jealous, only pleased and interested at his news. "Her family won't let us announce our engagement until she's through college or I'd have told you all sooner."

"Wonderful!" Squeak said, and at that moment Jack Reed cut in, to be followed a few moments later by Uncle Ed Singleton, whose wife was Mother's sister Augusta.

"Squeak. Honey!" he said, and kissed her on both cheeks before he started dancing. "To think that you should go and get yourself all grown up and beautiful in a few months. I suppose the next time Gussie and I come to Stapleton it'll be for your wedding."

"Alice next!" Squeak said, but in that instant she knew that without meaning to Uncle Ed had touched on the super-special magic of that evening. She *was* grown up. Suddenly and unexpectedly different, so that for the first time in her life she was as much at ease and sure of herself in evening clothes on the dance floor of a grownup party as she had been before in the village swimming pool or playing baseball after school.

It was a thrilling, heady discovery, and when Jube Carter cut in on her she had what seemed like outward as well as inward proof. "Golly, Squeak, I feel fierce about that Christmas Eve party," he said. "Being away all the time, I suppose I thought you were still Johnny's age."

"Oh, Jube, don't think of it," Squeak said, and as she beamed up at him the just-past Christmas might have been a hundred years ago. "You know Mum and Dad really like to have us home on Christmas Eve."

"It isn't the perfect time for a party," Jube agreed, "but next year if we have one at New Year's will you come?"

"I'd adore it," Squeak said. Another of the ushers cut in and she decided that perhaps growing up in a single evening was like love at first sight, unusual, infrequent, but definitely not impossible.

All too soon the party was over. Charlie and Sunny left shortly after midnight, but a half hour later, when Jube Carter and Tom took the girls home, they were sitting in the Bruces' living room. "Alice! Squeak!" Sunny hurried toward them. "A wedding present from Mrs. Hawks and Cliff. And the most adorable note. Cliff must have left them here when we were at the club."

For the first time all evening Squeak remembered her invitation to Cliff! She said nothing, but as she looked at the mahogany box which she remembered having seen in Mrs. Hawks' parlor her heart sank. "What a beauty." Alice stroked the gleaming wood. "Cliff certainly must have worked on rubbing it up."

Squeak didn't say a word as she read the note Sunny handed her. Mrs. Hawks had written, "Love and good wishes," on the face of her calling card and Cliff had scribbled on the back, "Sorry I couldn't get this to you sooner, but I didn't have a chance to work on it until today. All the best. Cliff."

Squeak swallowed the hard, dry knot that had formed in her throat and, looking up, realized that Alice was watching her. "Didn't you ask Cliff down for a Coke before the party?" she asked. "I thought I heard you as we were leaving for the rehearsal."

Squeak nodded, struggling for the light, casual tone of voice that had come to her so easily earlier in the evening. "Yes, I did, and then forgot all about it. Wasn't it dreadful of me?"

"Poor Cliff," Sunny said as she went out in the hall to say good night to Charlie. "We'll all have to make it up to him tomorrow."

"Oh, he'll live," Alice said and led the way upstairs. "It's just one of those things."

"He probably didn't count on coming," Squeak said as she followed Alice. "He was awfully offhand about answering."

A few moments later when she was alone in her room undressing for bed she knew that what she had just said was not true. Cliff had

144

counted on coming, as the delivery of his wedding present proved, and she had simply and cold-bloodedly forgotten him. I'll tell him I'm sorry first thing tomorrow, Squeak told herself, and scoured her teeth as though she could brush away the little blot on her conscience. He's always sounding off about how much he likes frankness.

But the next morning when Mrs. Bruce woke Squeak there was so much to be done getting the house ready for the wedding reception that she didn't even think of Cliff. She had been given the day off from school, but every minute of it was filled running errands, answering the telephone, and helping to rearrange the wedding presents.

Squeak was kept so busy with the jobs at hand that she didn't have a moment to herself until noon, when she went upstairs to wash up for lunch. And then she didn't think about Cliff, but about her blissful discovery at Sunny's party. It wasn't simply that she had been a success at a grownup dinner dance. What mattered was that through Tom Connaught and the others she had stumbled on a new sophistication, a maturity which even now twelve hours later left her feeling poised and invulnerable. I won't be fickle any more, she thought, and suddenly even the fantasies about her own future which she had so often indulged in seemed absurd. My feelings won't be easily hurt and Mum'll never have another chance to wonder if I'm six or sixteen!

15

I Give Thee My Troth   Mrs. Bruce had carefully arranged every detail so that there would not be any last-minute rush after luncheon. Even so it seemed to Squeak that the hours before the wedding evaporated without ever having existed and in no time at all it was quarter of four and Uncle Ed Singleton was driving Alice and herself and the other bridesmaids to the church.

"Jube and George Oakes both have cars," Alice said as they reached the front door, "and they'll drive us home. Jack Reed's driving Sunny and Charlie."

"Mighty good staff work," Uncle Ed said before he started back to the inn for Aunt Gussie. "But I'd trust your mother to make half a dozen weddings run smoothly. See you girls later."

Squeak nodded, and wriggling out of her coat, stood beside the other three girls in the vestry just as Mr. Bruce and Sunny, looking as remote and unfamiliar as a snow princess, came into the church.

This is it. This is Sunny's wedding. Squeak underlined the words in her own mind but even when the first tentative note of the Lohengrin wedding march trembled on the air she felt as unreal and detached as though she were an observer in a dream. Here comes the bride. Here comes the bride. Great swelling peals of organ music filled the familiar church and she and Alice moved slowly, rhythmically after the two other bridesmaids toward the altar.

At the front of the church they paused, separated in perfect time and turning, faced down the aisle toward Sunny, the white shimmering focus of their pageantry.

"Dearly beloved, we are gathered together here in the sight of God, and in the face of this company . . ." To Squeak the majestic words sounded as impersonal as organ music. ". . . to join together this Man and this Woman. . . ."

The service went on, but still Squeak felt queerly distant, apart.

"I, Sarah, take thee, Charles, to my wedded Husband . . ." Suddenly, as Sunny began her responses, Squeak heard and felt every word, every syllable. ". . . for better for worse, for richer for poorer . . ." Sunny's voice, low and reverent, was still so utterly and unself-consciously her own that Squeak's trancelike state gave way to an intense awareness. ". . . And thereto I give thee my troth."

As Sunny finished Squeak's heart pounded in a positive wave of love, of affirmation not simply for Sunny, for Charles, but to love itself, the holy estate of matrimony. *"And thereto I give thee my troth."*

When the organ broke into the gay, resounding strains of the Mendelssohn, Squeak was trembling from emotion and wondered how she could walk down the aisle. After the first step it was easy and as Tom Connaught fell into step beside her she was suddenly aware of her immediate surroundings. She heard the faint creak of Tom's shoes, smelled the fragrance of her own bouquet, and saw the smiling, familiar faces in the pews beyond her.

As they reached the back of the church she saw Cliff, looking strangely formal in his best blue suit with his red hair dark from wetting, standing in the last pew. She gave him a quick, contrite smile, but before she could catch his eye the procession swept her past him. A moment later she stood blinking in the bright wintry sunshine outside the church, and then hurried after Alice toward the car.

The first few minutes of the receiving line were fun, but as it wore on and there was no sign of Cliff she began to feel restless. Perhaps he was so hurt he went home, she thought. Just then she saw him coming up in the line beside Grandpa Lawrence.

"Cliff, I feel terrible!" she said the minute he was near her. "It was dreadful of me to forget asking you down before the Reeds' party."

"Doesn't matter a bit," Cliff said cheerfully, and beamed at Dr. Lawrence. "Your grandfather and I have just taken time out to go up to the shed to look at the books."

Squeak didn't have time to say anything more, but a few minutes later when the receiving line broke up and she was free to do as she liked she was still thinking about Cliff. The books today! she thought, and relief and irritation mixed and mingled within her. Of all the orginal one-track minds, his is the worst! Just then she heard her own name and turned to see Clare Clayton, impeccably dressed, in a gray faille afternoon dress, beckoning to her.

"Serena. Oh, Serena darling. I do want to talk to you. Those bridesmaids' dresses are easily the most becoming ones I've ever seen in my life."

Clare's voice was balm and Squeak turned to her beaming. "And wasn't Sunny darling? Wasn't she lovely?"

"Perfect!" Clare said, and they both turned so they could see Sunny and Charlie circulating among their wedding guests. "When you see a pair like that you're aware all over again that the marriage service is really a sacrament, a holy thing."

"That's just the way I felt!" Squeak said, and in that instant she

148

realized that Clare Clayton was the only person in the world who would really understand what had happened at the party the night before. "And I want to tell you, ask you, that is, about something that happened to me last evening." Squeak told her everything she had felt and thought and it was as easy to talk to Clare in the middle of the wedding reception as it would have been at Holly House. "And the wonderful thing is it's gone on all day today," she finished. "The being sure of myself, and not letting my feelings be hurt, or changing my mind in half a second."

Clare Clayton looked thoughtful and she was silent for so long that Squeak began to feel uneasy. "It will go on lasting, won't it?" she urged. "The wonderful part?"

"Some of it," Clare said finally, and Squeak, startled, heard the pity in her voice. "But not all of it, darling. You will never be invulnerable when your heart's involved. And learning to be one's real self is something we all keep on learning by stops and starts for the whole of life."

"You?" The one surprised word popped out of Squeak's mouth. "You?"

Clare laughed. "Oh yes. Oh, my yes. And change isn't necessarily foolish. Sometimes it's a sign of growth." Her beautifully manicured fingers touched one of the freesias in Squeak's bouquet. "A flower changes, Squeak, but you couldn't call it fickle."

"I know . . ." Squeak began, but as the eddying crowd wedged more closely around them she knew their snatched moment of privacy was over. "Still——"

Clare moved aside to let Harriet Tucker and George Oakes pass into the dining room, and when she and Squeak were thrown together again her voice was purely matter-of-fact. "Squeak, could you find Cliff Hawks for me? I was so cross to him the other day I've been feeling guilty ever since. I'm afraid he may have taken me literally when I said something hasty about wanting back the books."

"Oh, don't worry about Cliff," Squeak said just as Uncle Ed Singleton, looking plumper and rosier than ever, made his way toward them.

"Here you are!" Uncle Ed looked like a large, friendly pigeon in his wedding clothes. "That rascal Johnny said I'd find you here. And I do want you to introduce me. After all the years I've enjoyed Clare Post on the stage it's high time that I had the pleasure of meeting her."

Squeak turned. "Mrs. Clayton," she began, "this is my uncle, Edward Singleton."

"Call me Ed." Uncle Ed reached out and shook Clare's right hand with both of his. "This is a privilege, ma'am. A real privilege. And now I hope to learn that you are going back to Broadway in the future, the very near future."

"I am afraid not," Clare said, but although Squeak heard the warning chill in her voice Uncle Ed was completely oblivious.

"I'm one of your fans, you know. A real fan. I saw you first in *Peter's Planet*; that must have been, let me see, about the year Sunny was born, and followed you right along to *Valiant*. That was the last year of the war, when I went down to New York for a convention."

"Thank you," Clare said icily, but Uncle Ed was too wound up to stop.

"A great play. A fine play. Couldn't understand why you didn't take it on the road. We'd have welcomed you to Syracuse."

Just then Charles and Sunny moved behind them on their way to the dining room. Squeak didn't see them, but she was intensely aware of the sudden hush as smiling wedding guests moved aside to let them pass. And then Clare spoke. "I never had any intention of taking *Valiant* or any other play to Syracuse," she said. "Never."

Squeak saw the surprised look on Uncle Ed's face and felt the soft flip of fur on her bare arm as Clare pulled her stole more closely around her. She was dimly aware that Cliff and Grandpa Lawrence had come up to join them, but before she could say a single word Clare Clayton had turned and, only pausing to shake hands with Mrs. Bruce, left the house. Uncle Ed ran his hand through his silver-gray hair so that the back of it stuck up like Johnny's. "Well, I'll be shot," he said. "Somehow I put my big foot into trouble."

There was an instant of silence, suddenly broken by strains of "The Blue Danube" and a burst of applause as Sunny and Charlie went into the dining room. "What in the world did I say?" Uncle Ed said ruefully. "Squeak, honey, what did I do?"

Squeak's mouth opened and closed, but it was Cliff Hawks who answered him. "I don't think it was anything to do with you, Mr. Singleton. You see, her husband was killed at the end of her last play and I guess she can't stand having it mentioned. Mrs. Frostgate was like that about her son."

But Clare isn't—she doesn't—the unspoken words beat through Squeak's mind like a pulse, but before she could say anything Uncle Ed had moved off toward the punch bowl and Grandpa Lawrence was talking. "I was amazed at the things Cliff showed me up at the shed," he said, and it took Squeak a long moment to realize that he meant the cobbler's shed. "And I congratulate both of you on the work you've done. And now I was wondering if you could come up to New York and lunch with me next Saturday at Dragonetti's. Cliff said he'd like to do it and maybe go to a book auction and check up on some of the bookstores the same day."

"That'd be fine, wonderful," Squeak found her tongue just as Uncle Ed rejoined them.

"I wish I'd gone to you for briefing, Dr. Lawrence," Uncle Ed said. "I'm sure you Manhattanites know how to handle prima donnas but it's too much for us homespun Upstaters."

Dr. Lawrence smiled and his keen old eyes scanned the room around him. "Too bad there were fireworks," he said, and then, looking down at Squeak, he added, "I'm interested that your mother invited the lady at all. At Christmas dinner I was under the impression that you'd only just met."

"Oh, we've seen something of her because of the books," Squeak said, and suddenly tempted to be free of the whole thing, she rushed on. "And you know how Sunny is. I guess Mum and Dad are lucky they didn't have to build on an extension to take care of all the people she's sorry for."

Squeak's voice sounded high and false, but neither Grandpa nor Uncle Ed noticed it. "Of course. It's just like Sunny." Uncle Ed lifted his punch glass in the direction of the dining room. "Bless the girl."

Just then Johnny rushed into the room with the flower broken off from his buttonhole and his best shirt pulled loose from his trousers. "Grandpa! Squeak. All of you. C'mon to the dining room. Sunny's going to cut the cake."

Squeak turned to follow him and found herself facing Cliff. She saw his amused expression and remembered that he had been in the hall when she had asked Sunny to invite Clare Clayton to the wedding. She waited until Grandpa and Uncle Ed, with Johnny between them, had gone off to the dining room, and then snapped, "Well, what's so funny? Clare was just plain rude to Uncle Ed and you know it."

Cliff's smile grew wider and more irritating. "I wasn't thinking about Clare at all," he said. "I was thinking about you."

"Skip it!" Squeak said, and hurried off to the dining room.

She managed to avoid Cliff for most of the rest of the reception, but for a long while his "I was thinking about you" hung in the air like the Cheshire cat's grin. Gradually as the afternoon wore on her crossness went too and by the time Sunny and Charles hurried out through a storm of confetti she realized that, considering Cliff's opportunities for teasing, he had actually been generous.

By eight o'clock most of the guests had left and the ushers and bridesmaids drifted together in a corner and began offering and comparing plans for the rest of the evening. Finally Mary Reed's suggestion that they go down to Blake's Grille for a late spaghetti supper won and Alice gave a loud gasp of relief. "Wonderful," she said, and took off her slippers. "If I had to go anywhere and dance my feet would come off."

"Me too," Harriet said, and leaned against George Oakes for support. "What a business."

Jack Reed began counting how many wanted to go, and then when he came to Alice stopped. "Want to ask anybody else?"

"Can't be bothered," Alice said, and at that moment Squeak saw a sudden golden chance to square herself.

"I might," she said, and hurried out of the room to find Cliff Hawks. She caught up with him just as he and the Harris family were saying good-by to her parents. "Cliff. Cliff, wait a second," she called, and, when he had followed her just out of the Harrises' hearing, hurried on: "How about coming over to Blake's with us for some spaghetti?"

Cliff only looked at her and as the Harrises moved on toward the door he shook his head. "Sorry, I can't," he said, and then, calling out, "I'm coming!" dashed after Lyb Harris.

Squeak was as startled as though he had slapped her. Her eyes stung, but she threw back her head as she went over to the other room and said loudly, "Oh, let's not ask anybody else. We've had enough of crowds to last us for ages."

"Good with me," Jack Reed said.

"In fact perfect," Seth Reed said, and as he moved over beside Squeak she resolved not to think again about Cliff. Let him go after Lyb, she thought. I certainly don't care.

She did her best to throw herself into the party at Blake's, and to be funny and amusing so that no one could guess that she had been turned down. The crowd laughed good-naturedly at her wisecracks and Seth Reed acted as though she were the wittiest girl in creation, but even so there was none of last night's spell about this evening. By the time they drove home she felt drained and dull and her face was stiff from smiling. As she followed Alice up through the silent house to her parents' bedroom she couldn't think of anything except how glad she was that the evening was finally over.

"Did you have fun, darling?" Mum looked at her curiously. "You look absolutely exhausted."

"I feel fine!" Squeak stiffened instantly. "And the spaghetti was super. Cliff Hawks really missed something."

"He certainly did," Alice said, and yawned. "But don't rub it in. He was going down to New York to spend Sunday with his father and his new stepmother. I heard him ask the Harrises for a lift to the train and he sounded about as cheerful as if he was going to have a tooth out."

Squeak managed to go on to her own room without saying a word, but as she undressed she was still tingling with relief. Cliff hadn't fallen for Lyb. Of course not. It was simply stubborn loyalty and pride that had kept him from mentioning the visit which he must have dreaded. It's exactly like him, she thought, as she stretched out in bed. She lay quite still, smiling up into the darkness and her mind moved freely, happily back over the day. Sunny. Darling Sunny. And Charlie. Quiet and handsome in his blue uniform with his arm protectively around his wife as they rushed toward the car through a hailstorm of rice and confetti. Squeak shut her eyes while the wedding sights and sounds, the very smell of flowers drifted before her. It was only as she turned over, more than half asleep, that she remembered how Cliff had looked standing erect and quiet in the back of the church. And then from nowhere at all she heard the echo of Clare Clayton's beautiful voice when she had said, "You will never be invulnerable when your heart's involved."

16

Workaday Sunday The day after Sunny's wedding was busy for the Bruces. For once on a Saturday no one was allowed to drift down to breakfast to help himself when and how they pleased, but the whole family, in varying stages of sleepiness, ate together at half-past eight. By nine Mrs. Hilsen had arrived and was running the vacuum cleaner through the hall as though each grain of rice or fleck of confetti were a personal offense. Mrs. Bruce and Alice began rewrapping wedding presents that were to be stored until after Charlie was out of the Army, and Mr. Bruce, Squeak, and Johnny set to work putting furniture back in place.

By the early part of the afternoon the house looked normal again. Alice went upstairs to pack to go back to college the next day. Johnny went outside and Mr. and Mrs. Bruce settled down to finish up the wedding presents together while Mrs. Hilsen cleaned the kitchen. Only Squeak had no idea of what she wanted to do next. She wandered into the girls' room and found that Alice had appropriated every inch of Sunny's bed and bureau for her own packing. "Go get my ski socks, will you?" she asked without looking up from her suitcase. "I think they're in the laundry."

"Who was your bond servant last year?" Squeak used the ancient formula of their childhood, but since she had nothing else to do she went downstairs after the socks. As she passed through the

156

kitchen Mrs. Hilsen threw two faded bridesmaids' bouquets into the rubbish can and clamped down the top as though she relished her work. Squeak hurried out again, trying not to think that the wilted flowers had looked reproachful. She glanced out of the library window and saw that Johnny was using the crepe-paper snow man Harriet Tucker and Mary Reed had given him as a target for his slingshot. She averted her eyes from the torn, dirtied mass of white and, turning back into the library, picked up the photograph of Sunny which had been taken six months ago, at the time of her engagement. It's too soon, it's disgusting. They're all so callous. Squeak fumbled to put her incoherent sentiments into words. Just then the telephone rang and she dropped the picture face-down as she rushed to answer.

It was Clare Clayton, sounding brisk and businesslike at the other end. "I'm moving into the cottage on Wednesday," she said, "and I've found some books of my own that I sent up here before I went to England and I thought perhaps you and Cliff would like to have them to add to the others."

"Oh, we'd love them," Squeak said, and Clare answered, "Good. If you can come up here late this afternoon to pick out the ones you want, I'll drive you and the books home on my way out to dinner. And we could have a cup of tea in the meantime."

"Thanks. I'd love it." Squeak hung up the receiver just as Alice came down in search of the socks. "I'm going to Clare Clayton's for tea," she said, and, as Alice's eyebrows lifted, hurried on defensively. "There isn't more tidying to do around here. You're not helping Mum. You're packing."

"I wasn't thinking of tidying." Alice set Sunny's picture upright as she spoke. "I was thinking of Cliff Hawks and the books. I thought once Sunny's wedding was over you were going to hump yourself to do your share of the work."

"Clare wants me to pick out some more books today," Squeak said crushingly. "And since when have you been so worried about Cliff?"

"Oh, I'm not worried," Alice said, but the words rang in Squeak's ear like a challenge.

"If you must know, I'm going to type all the penciled lists we've made before he gets home tomorrow," she said, and didn't add that the idea had just come into her mind that moment.

Alice started to answer, but just then Mr. and Mrs. Bruce came into the library and Squeak told them about her invitation. "Fine," Mr. Bruce said, and started out toward the garage with his armload of packages. "I'll drop you off when I take Mrs. Hilsen home."

"Good," Squeak said, and as Alice picked up her socks and started upstairs, turned to her mother. "There isn't anything else you want me to do around here, is there, Mum?"

"No, darling, not a thing," Mrs. Bruce said. "I'm going upstairs to have a bath and lie down myself. Having the wedding over and Sunny gone is suddenly flattening."

"Isn't it, though?" Squeak said, and told her mother how she had felt about the flowers and crepe-paper snow man. Unlike Clare Clayton at the wedding reception, Mrs. Bruce's answer was crisp and immediate. "No use mixing sentimentality with real feeling," she said. "The best thing to do is to get going on the next job, and I hope this week you'll really be able to help Cliff with the books. He's been wonderful about slaving up at the shed by himself."

They can only think about Cliff, Squeak fumed, but she knew both Alice and her mother had been right and, after lugging the family typewriter up to her own room, settled down to typing the lists in the hour and a half that was left before going to Holly House.

The work was absorbing and although Squeak was an inexpert

typist the difference in looks between her hunt-and-peck efforts and the scribbled lists was distinctly heartening. I'll be able to finish it by tomorrow evening, she decided, and, as she thought of how pleased and surprised Cliff would be, gloated inwardly. Of course he won't say a thing, she warned herself, but somehow that didn't seem to matter, and when her father shouted, "All aboard," from the bottom of the stairs she raced down after him with a light heart.

It was only after he had dropped her off at the stone lions that it occurred to her that it might be embarrassing to see Clare so soon after the episode with Uncle Ed. She'll never mention it, Squeak encouraged herself as she rang the doorbell. She's much too smooth. A moment later, as Clare Clayton opened the door, Squeak found out that she was entirely wrong.

"I'm so ashamed of myself," Clare said even before she led the way out of the hall. "Your uncle only meant to be kind and I was absolutely boorish. I can't stand hearing anyone even mention *Valiant* or my acting in it."

"It doesn't matter," Squeak said uncomfortably, and followed Clare into the library, which looked bleak and unfamiliar now that all of the books and most of the furniture had been removed. "Uncle Ed's a very jolly, understanding sort of person. He's a little like Mrs. Frostgate in that."

"Why do the good and wise and *steadying* people have to die?" Clare burst out. "I'd never have behaved like that while Basil was alive."

"I'm—I'm so terribly sorry." Squeak ached to say the right, the comforting words, but all she could think of was, "And I'm just positive Uncle Ed doesn't really mind."

"You're a darling!" Clare Clayton said, and began to make the tea. "And I wish you'd known my Basil. One of the reasons why I went to England was to see the people he'd been with during the war."

Squeak took the cup Clare handed her and suddenly her Enid and Geraint theory seemed unutterably silly. Basil Clayton had never wronged his wife. Instead he had loved her so tenderly that the theater, which had been their joint life, seemed empty to his widow. She looked up to speak, but now Clare smiled at her apologetically. "What an old crepe hanger I am," she said. "I ask you over for tea, and then depress you almost to tears. I'm worse than a caller I had who used the word 'late,' meaning dead, as often as most people use Mr. or Mrs."

Squeak grinned and instantly Clare Clayton pursed her lips and arched her little finger away from her cup in artificial refinement. "Ah, delicious, Mrs.—er—Clayton. May I presume to ask where you purchase your tea? The late Mrs. Frostgate did not, I believe, trade at Geiseler's."

"Mrs. Apsley!" Squeak laughed so that it was hard to speak. "But when did she call on you?"

"Thursday," Clare said, and now her mobile mouth was humorously grim. "And don't think she didn't make it entirely plain that she was only here in her official capacity as one of the church visiting committee. She herself had never 'mingled socially with Bohemians,' she told me, but that didn't stop her from prying into every angle of my leaving this house and moving into the cottage. At one point I thought she was going to insist on seeing the drains!"

"I'll bet!" Squeak said. "It sounds exactly like her."

"I think she was secretly disappointed not to find me smoking marijuana," Clare said. "But now come and look at the books. Miss Petersen was shocked because I didn't take time to dust them before I called you."

"Cliff and I have turned into expert book dusters," Squeak said.

"We just leave the books alone and they dust themselves while we go over them, but we wouldn't tell that to Mrs. Hilsen or Miss Petersen."

There were nearly fifty books, mostly novels and poetry of ten years or more ago, in two orange crates in the empty dining room. Squeak began to go over them while Clare went upstairs to change, and found that she was automatically assigning them to the categories she and Cliff had worked out between them. There were none of the hopeless or for-pulping-only variety and when Clare came down again, ready to drive over to Wilton, Squeak looked up. "My guess is that these are all salable," she said briskly, and then, as Clare reached for the Everyman edition of *Leaves of Grass,* which was nearest to her, wondered if she had been too abrupt.

"Don't you want to keep some of these?" she asked anxiously, but Clare only shook her head and began carrying the books out to the car.

"I haven't even thought about them for ten years," she said, "and the cottage bookshelves are full of things I want to read, so it would be silly to dawdle over these. There's no point mixing sentimentality with the real joy of reading."

Squeak said nothing as they loaded the car and it wasn't until they turned on to the valley road that it occurred to her that what Clare had just said was almost exactly parallel to what Mum had said about getting on to the next job earlier in the afternoon.

It was too muddy to drive up to the shed, so they unloaded the books in the Bruces' garage. "Good-by, and thanks loads," Squeak said as Clare slid back behind the wheel again.

"Thank you," Clare said, and reached out and touched Squeak's shoulder. "And the next time you see your uncle tell him I'm abject."

She drove off and Squeak stood looking after her car until the taillight disappeared. She's a darling, Squeak thought. I bet the scandal Grandpa couldn't remember was simply that when she left the stage the people who wanted her to stay spread a lot of rotten stories without a word of truth in them.

Squeak went to bed early that night and woke up the next morning feeling rested and ready for work. The family went off to church and she stuck at typing out her lists until it was time for Sunday dinner. "I've almost finished typing our lists," she said as her father started carving the roast. "And even with the new books from Clare we'll be all finished by next week."

"Cliff must have slaved," Alice said. "The last time I went up to the shed you had plenty left to do."

"That's right," Squeak said evenly, and wondered why only yesterday she had been ready to bite every time anyone mentioned how much Cliff had done. I was just feeling guilty, she decided, and, as soon as she could after luncheon, went back to her typing. She finished at a little before four and went downstairs to say goodby to Alice. "Are you sure you don't want to drive over to Stamford with us?" Mother asked. "We thought we'd stop in at Turner's Tavern for supper on the way home."

"No, thanks," Squeak said. "I'll scramble eggs or something. I still have a lot of work to do here."

"I think you're nuts," Johnny said, and scuttled after his parents to the waiting car. "Going to Turner's is fun."

Squeak turned to say good-by to Alice and, when she saw her face, knew she had guessed that there was another reason why she had not wanted to leave the house. "Give Cliff the Hawk my love," Alice said dryly, and, before Squeak could say a word, gave her a quick hug and hurried out to the car.

Alice always has to be so smart, Squeak thought, and went upstairs to change into dungarees and a heavy sweater. After all, with the new books and the lists to show Cliff why shouldn't I want to be here? She went downstairs and started toward the garage when it occurred to her for the first time that perhaps Cliff was not coming back until late and wouldn't be able to stop in until after school on Monday. He should have told me when he was going and when he was coming back, she thought, and at that moment a telephone-repair truck came to a grinding stop by the mailbox. She turned, wondering, and heard Cliff's familiar voice call out, "Thanks for the lift." A moment later she saw him running up the rise, his bright hair flamboyantly red against the dull winter sky. "Hi, Cliff!" she called out. "I was just thinking you wouldn't be back until tomorrow."

"Not a chance!" Cliff looked more puckishly pleased with himself than ever. "I took the 2:30 train from New York and I've been getting practically free taxi service hitchhiking ever since."

"Did you have fun? Was it a good week end?"

"O.K.," Cliff said. "But now let's see the books Clare Clayton gave us. Anything good?"

Squeak stared at him. "Cliff Hawks, how did you know about those books? Did Clare tell you about them?"

Cliff grinned. "Not a word. But Miss Petersen said plenty when I dropped my bag at Gran's just now, especially about how dirty they were and how it was queer that an educated woman like Mrs. Clayton didn't appreciate real Scandinavian cleanliness."

"Boy, I can hear her," Squeak said, and led the way to the garage. "We'll have to carry them up to the shed. It was too muddy to drive up there yesterday."

"Leave that to Charles Atlas Hawks," Cliff said, and swung one of the crates up onto his shoulders. "You go get your key and I'll meet you down here when I come back for the second load."

"Sure you can manage?" Squeak asked, but Cliff had started

toward the shed, so she hurried into the house and picked up her list and the key.

Cliff was just reaching for the second crate when she came down again. "Put that down and look!" she said, and waved the typewritten lists in front of him. "If I don't get buttered up for this I'm going to blow my top."

Cliff looked at the lists page by page, and whistled. "Squeak, this is terrific!" he said. "Supersensational. And now that the wedding's over and I have that blank week end behind me we can really go places."

"Good," Squeak said, and reached a handful of books out of the crate as Cliff hoisted it upward. "Let's go."

"You really did a knockout piece of work," Cliff said, and Squeak hugged the books to her as she followed him to the shed. Cliff was pleased, really pleased, and what was even more important was that now it was manifestly clear that the reason why Cliff hadn't mentioned the week end ahead of time was because he had dreaded it.

Cliff unlocked the door and let Squeak in ahead of him. "Golly, it's freezing in here," she said, and reached for the matches. "Much worse than outside."

"Cold as the forsaken tomb!" Cliff sang as he hauled in the other crate of books. "We'll both get icicle whiskers."

Squeak lit the oil stove and as she straightened up saw Cliff stop in the middle of a teamster's warming. His arms dropped to his sides and he sprang over to the shelves like a terrier to a rathole. "Squeak! Have you or Alice or any of your family been up here since I showed your grandfather around?"

"No, of course not. Why?" Squeak asked, but as she stared at the shelves she too was aware, without entirely knowing how, that the books had been shifted about. "Didn't you leave the books this way?"

"No! I did not!" Cliff jerked a paper marker from a book of plays and showed Squeak where it had been creased when it had been pushed in between the pages a second time. "I put in these markers Thursday night," he said. "They were just the way I'd left them when I showed your grandfather around on Friday. So whoever it was that touched them has been here since then. And they weren't making any Fox Fur rush job of it, either!"

"But how could anyone get in? I've had my key in the back of my jewelry case for the past week," Squeak said, and then, as she saw Cliff's red, embarrassed face, guessed the answer. "With your key?"

Cliff nodded dumbly. "I—I always leave it on the hall table," he said. "Grandma and Miss Petersen pass it every time they go to the dining room."

"But they wouldn't come down here. Your grandmother's too lame and Miss Petersen wouldn't take the Gutenberg Bible if it was dusty."

"I know that. The point is Miss Petersen might have handed the key to someone who wanted to come in here when we weren't around."

"To Clare?" Squeak burst out. "But that's crazy. She's just given us all these extra books."

"I didn't say Clare," Cliff began, and Squeak interrupted him.

"Well, I should hope not!" Then, as she saw Cliff's unhappy face, her anger faded. "Cliff. Cliff, what's the trouble?"

He looked around the shed and shrugged sheepishly. "This," he said. "Even if nothing's taken it's going to be terribly hard to finish up by next Saturday."

"Maybe Mum and Dad would help," Squeak began. Then she remembered what had happened the last time she had told her family about the shed being entered and took a step toward him.

"We won't tell a soul. We'll handle this ourselves, Cliff. The two of us!"

Cliff's head lifted and his arms went around her waist. "You darling," he said, and his dark eyes glowed. "You darling!"

Squeak reached forward for his kiss. His cool, young cheek met hers, but before their lips touched he pulled himself away. Squeak stared after him, as startled and hurt as though he had slapped her. "Cliff—Cliff——"

"I couldn't help it," he muttered, and as he faced the books she saw his neck and ears turn a hot, angry red. "I keep forgetting that there's extra work to do and it's all my fault."

17

The Bookstores   Squeak sat still, feeling numb and hurt as Cliff counted the books. "None gone," he said finally, and his voice sounded entirely satisfied. "Twice somebody's been over these books and nothing was taken either time. What are they looking for?"

"I don't know and I care less!" Squeak said furiously. What did books, any books matter, compared to what had happened between Cliff and herself? She fiddled miserably with the book nearest to her and Cliff took a step toward her.

"Squeak," he said. "I can't talk. I'm no good at explaining. We've got to get through this job first before——"

"Oh, I understand perfectly!" Squeak said, and now pride swept away every other feeling. "After all, the whole point of my coming up here this afternoon was to try to get finished by the end of this week."

"That's it! That's the point exactly!" Cliff's obvious enthusiasm was as unexpected as a splash of cold water—and nearly as bracing.

"We'd better start going over Clare's books," Squeak said, and reached for the Whitman, which Clare had dropped back on the top of the crate. "This is *Leaves of Grass* in the Everyman edition." She reached over to drop it with the other reprints, when unexpectedly Cliff took the book out of her hand and thumbed through it until he found what he had wanted.

"Did you ever read *Song of Myself?*" he asked, and when Squeak didn't answer he began to read aloud:

". . . for me mine male and female,
For me those that have been boys and that love woman,
For me the man that is proud and feels how it
stings to be slighted,
For me the sweet heart and the old maid, for me
mothers and the mothers of mothers."

Squeak turned away from the glaring light of the single overhead bulb. What was Cliff trying to tell her? That when he thought of love at all it was in terms of the whole world, that when he had reached out toward her a little while ago it might just as well have been Johnny, or Clare Clayton, or Miss Petersen? Or was he trying to say something entirely different?

She looked up at him just as he closed the book and his face was expressionless. "I never read poetry," he said. "But one of the masters up at Yardley read that aloud and I just happened to remember it. I thought you might like it."

"It's very good," Squeak said, and managed to keep her voice impersonal. "And now shall we go on to the next book? It's *The King's Henchman,* by Edna St. Vincent Millay."

From then on they worked without stopping until they heard a car drive up to the house, and a few minutes later Mr. Bruce came up to the shed. "Still at it?" he said. "I hope you took time off for a good supper?"

"We haven't stopped for a thing." Cliff sprang up from the stool he had perched on. "I should have thought about Squeak's being hungry."

"She would have thought of it herself if she'd been starving," Mr. Bruce said. "But now you two better come down and have something to eat, and then I'll run you home."

Cliff looked questioningly at Squeak, but she only turned toward the door, and after he had locked it and handed her the key he spoke to Mr. Bruce. "Thanks a lot, but I think I'd better get along to Grandma's. This is my lucky day on rides and I'll probably pick up a lift in no time flat."

"Not at this time of night," Mr. Bruce said. "So I'll drive you home now. Want to come, Squeak?"

"No, thanks," Squeak said. "I've some homework to do and tomorrow's Monday."

As they drove off Squeak went into the kitchen and helped herself to some cold cereal. When she had finished she went upstairs to do her homework. By the time she reached the last page of her French she was so tired she could hardly see the print for yawning, but once she was actually in bed sleep was a long time coming.

"I don't love him. I don't love him." Squeak said the words over and over to herself as she twisted and turned, trying to think of something, anything but the look on Cliff's face when he had pulled away from her.

She tried to conjure up school, last summer's holiday trip, Lyb Harris and other friends, but their images stayed as flat and lifeless as cardboard, and when she tried to think about "The Idyll" it seemed as pathetic and embarrassing as an outgrown toy.

Finally her mind moved on to Sunny and suddenly she could almost see her, not as she had seen her last, not at the wedding, but late last summer in the pale blue linen dress she had worn so often, and Sunny was saying, "When you find the right person, darling, then you'll know."

Squeak pushed herself upright in bed. I have found the right person and I know I love him, but he doesn't love me. Now what do I do? There was no answer and she lay back again, still wakeful, but at least freed of the itching torment of trying to pretend even to herself.

I wish I could talk it over with someone, she thought. Not the family, not Clare, certainly none of the girls at school. She stretched out her legs and it occurred to her that if her problem were about anyone else she would go far to hear Cliff's crisp, honest, and unexpectedly observant answer. The idea of asking what to do, when you hadn't been kissed, of the very boy who hadn't kissed you was so grotesque that Squeak grinned in spite of herself and settled more easily under the sheets and blankets. She remembered his reading the Whitman, and now it seemed possible that he was trying to tell her that if he didn't love her in the way she wanted to be loved he didn't love anybody else that way either. That's something, she thought, not much, but something. If I can get through this week I can make him love me. He needs the money, so he's hipped on finishing the books. If I can get through this week . . . She closed her eyes and once more she saw Cliff, but now his head was back and he was laughing with the pencil sticking out from his ear at a rakish angle. She remembered his unexpectedly breaking out into: " 'Oh, you can't go to heaven in powder and paint,' " and smiled to herself. And in a little while she slept.

The next morning Squeak began to think about Cliff even before she turned off the alarm clock, and to worry about what he had or had not meant. I'll have to wait until next week, she told herself. Next week everything will be easy. Now I have to do the job at hand and keep my mind on that. She began to dress, and then, propping her history book on the bureau, forced herself to read the underlined passages while she brushed her hair.

Three quarters of an hour later, as the school bus slowed down to take her on, she saw Cliff's red head before the bus came to a full stop, and for an instant her courage failed. It's going to be harder than I thought—her heart seemed to pound out the words by itself—it's going to be much harder. She hesitated for a fraction of a second, and then stepped onto the bus holding her head high. "You look full of pep this morning," the bus driver said, and she smiled back at him, more determined than ever to stick to her plan for the week.

Cliff waved to her and pointed to the seat he had saved at the back of the bus, but she only held up her French book to him, and settled down in the one single seat and began to study. If I help him all this week and we finish everything he's bound to feel differently about me, she told herself, and struggled to concentrate on irregular verbs.

From then on the days of the week went by in a new and exhausting pattern. Both at school and during the afternoons at the cobbler's shed Squeak threw herself into her work so that she had no time to think of her own feelings. By the time she had finished her homework after supper she was so tired that she could hardly wait to go to bed, but it was only after she had gone through the formula of rereading the passage from Whitman which Cliff had read to her, and then reassured herself that he didn't love anyone else, that she slept.

By Saturday morning, when Mrs. Bruce drove Squeak up to the Center on the way to the station, she felt limp and depressed from overwork, but Cliff, who was waiting for them outside of his grandmother's picket fence, looked brisker and more cheerful than ever. "Great day to go to New York," he said, and sniffed the cold air like a beagle. "Couldn't get nearly as much done if we'd had rain or another snowstorm. With any luck we'll get the whole book business settled by this evening."

"I wouldn't count on making too much money," Mrs. Bruce said. "Mrs. Tappen tells me secondhand books are a drug on the market."

"Yes, she told us that too," Cliff said. "And so did the bookstore people I saw down in Stamford. But I'm counting on Mrs. Frostgate not to let us down."

"I think you'll be very lucky if you get fifty dollars," Mrs. Bruce said, and Squeak glanced curiously at Cliff. Was it possible that he still took the word "treasure" literally and wouldn't or couldn't realize that the old lady had obviously meant the joy of reading, which had played such a big part in her own long life? She said nothing and a few minutes later Mrs. Bruce dropped them at the station and they boarded the train.

Squeak opened the copy of *Seventeen* that she had brought to read on the way and Cliff leaned back with a sigh of pure pleasure. "Boy, oh boy, have I been waiting for today." He turned to Squeak, his eyes sparkling and his mouth twisted in the grin that she had once thought cocky and now found melting. "All love is wonder." The line Squeak had read on Christmas Eve popped into her mind, but she pushed it away from her for more practical things. "Cliff, you're crazy if you still think we're going to make a fortune," she said, and felt as though she were disillusioning Johnny. "Mrs. Frostgate meant bookish treasures. Finding new authors and stories. That sort of thing."

Cliff's quick, supple fingers moved instinctively toward his pocket. "For you, maybe," he said, and as he checked the contents of his wallet Squeak knew he had brought his letter along. "But for old Uncle Clifford she meant something else again. Oh golly, Squeak, I feel better. This last week up at the shed I've felt as though we were shoving icebergs around in the dark."

"You felt that way. You! But that's the way I've felt and all because of Sun——" Squeak checked herself before she had finished the sentence, and ended up lamely. "All I know is that I've never plugged so hard at one thing before in my life."

"Maybe that's what Mrs. Frostgate intended. To test us and tease us. It would be exactly like her."

"I don't understand!" Squeak said. "And remember you've read my letter from her, but I've never read yours."

Once more Cliff's hand moved toward his pocket. He put back his head and laughed so that the people across the aisle turned to look at him. "That's part of it," he said when he could speak at all. "And I'll bet my shirt Mrs. F. had the whole thing planned."

Squeak's eyes pricked with tears and she lifted her magazine to hide her face, but Cliff pushed it away. "Squeak, listen. I'll show it to you the minute we've finished with the books, and then you'll understand. About Mrs. Frostgate, and the treasure, and us, and everything. You've got to believe me!"

His voice was husky with feeling and as Squeak looked back at him hope soared in her heart. "I do," she said. "I really do."

They talked very little for the rest of the train ride, but for the first time in six days Squeak felt gay and lighthearted. I feel the way I did at the party before Sunny's wedding, she thought as Cliff guided her expertly through the maze of the subway. But this is an awful queer sort of a dance.

They left the subway at Eighth Street and as Cliff took out their typewritten list and pointed up Fourth Avenue it was clear he had planned the day like a military campaign. "We'll begin with these stores here," he said. "And then go to a couple on Fifth Avenue and maybe have time to see if we can get any free advice at the library before we meet your grandfather. Have you anything else you want to do?"

Squeak, who had thought of spending her Christmas money on a nylon sweater, turned away from the beautiful tailored suit and the glamorous dinner dress in Wanamaker's window. "Even if I did I wouldn't dare mention it," she said. "Lead on, Simon Legree."

They walked into the first store and found it was nearly empty. Cliff went off to the back office to speak to the proprietor and Squeak looked around her curiously.

The place was large and poorly lighted. The books, except for one table marked, "Review Copies," which still had on their bright paper jackets, were drab and dingy-looking. The air was stuffy with book dust and steam heat and, as Squeak wandered over to a table of ten-cent books and saw a battered copy of Milton and two bound volumes of sermons that reminded her of the books that had belonged to Mr. Frostgate, she felt suddenly depressed. She had an idea now of the dirty, backbreaking work that went into sorting old books and knew that if the store sold them for ten cents they probably would only pay a cent or two. Still the first editions might be worth something. She wandered on to other tables where the books were both more interesting and more expensive and, pulling out a collection of short stories, read the first page of the *Luck of Roaring Camp* before Cliff came up to her. "Back at your old tricks?" he said, and led the way outside before she could ask what they had been offered.

"Twenty-three dollars and fifty cents, delivered!" he told her the moment they were on the pavement, and now even his shoulders looked discouraged. "That means we'd be getting the whole of about five cents an hour for our work."

Squeak, who had been doing some figuring of her own, nodded, and, as an idea came to her, turned to Cliff. "Listen! Lookit! Did you tell them that someone has been interested enough to sneak in to look at those books when we weren't around? There must be something valuable?"

"You can tell 'em," Cliff said as they crossed the avenue to another bookshop. "Just now, when I pointed out that we'd checked on all those first editions, the man practically patted me on the head and told me to go back to playing marbles."

Squeak said nothing, but two minutes later when they had handed over their list in the next store and she had told the man their story she saw Cliff's point. The bookstore man merely glanced at their list before handing it back to Cliff. "I guess you two have had a lot of fun," he said patronizingly. "There's nothing better than a mystery when you're young."

"But it wasn't fun," Squeak said furiously. "It just made a lot of extra work and we'd slaved already. But it proves that someone, two people, wanted something badly enough to steal it."

The man shrugged. "Thought you said nothing was taken? If you ask me it was just some of your neighbors indulging their curiosity or maybe hoping to pick up some old postage stamps or something like that."

"There weren't any valuable covers at all," Cliff said. "The old lady who owned these books tore off all her stamps to give me when I was a kid." At that moment his mouth opened and shut fishily as though he'd just thought of something unbelievable but obvious. Squeak started to ask him what it was, but Cliff had already collected himself and asked the bookseller how much he was prepared to offer.

The man grimaced. "Twenty dollars. Maybe twenty-five if your books check with your list."

"No sale," Cliff said shortly, and fairly hauled Squeak out of the store.

"What is it?" she asked the minute they were out on the street. "What did you think of all of a sudden?"

"Me. Us. The books," Cliff said incoherently. "I've been a dope. "Both Fox Fur and whoever came that second time may have been

175

more interested in what was *in the books* than the books themselves."

"But there weren't any stamps. Except perfectly ordinary two- and three-cent ones. You said so yourself."

"Letters, notes, jottings. Maybe even some of those old clippings. Any of that stuff just might be priceless."

Squeak stared at him. A lightninglike thought struck and kindled in her mind, and she started forward. "Autographs!" she burst out. "Of course that's it. But what shall we do now? Skip trying to sell the books until we can collect and go over every scrap and leaf of paper there may be up at the shed?"

Cliff shook his head. "Of course not," he said. "We'll go ahead and make the best deal we can while we're here and then go through the books tonight. You were bright to keep that old prayer book."

"I didn't keep it out of brightness. I kept it because I felt as though I'd known the girl who owned it. But, Cliff, Clifford Hawks, wouldn't it be wonderful if there was an autograph that was worth mints?"

Cliff stared at her, started to speak, thought better of it, and guided her into the biggest bookstore on the avenue. Once more he handed over their list to a man in the back office while Squeak wandered around the tables and counters in front. She was too absorbed now to browse, and simply read an occasional title mechanically while her mind explored a whole new field of glory. Autographs. Treasure. Wasn't it Button Gwinnett who had signed the Declaration of Independence and whose signature, almost unknown, was worth thousands upon thousands of dollars? She stared at a familiar-looking book on the dollar counter for a full minute before she realized that it was Burns Mantle's *Best Plays for 1944–45.*

She turned eagerly to *Valiant* and had just found a picture of

176

Clare Clayton in a long evening dress when Cliff came up beside her. "Look!" she said excitedly. "Look at what I've found."

"She certainly looks a lot older now," Cliff said. He took the book out of Squeak's hands and carried it over to the back office. A moment later he came back and pushed it toward her. "It's yours," he said. "I just bought it."

The hope which had started in Squeak's heart on the train roared forward in a great shining wave. "Cliff, you shouldn't," she said. "But thanks a million. I've wanted to see this for ages."

"So have I," Cliff said grimly. "It won't tell us much, but at least it will tell us something about Clare Clayton and her last play. From now on in I'm going to make it my business to find out every single thing I can about that lady."

The smile faded from Squeak's face. "Cliff, you're crazy. You can't think Clare got your key from Miss Petersen. We went into all of that!"

"I didn't say anything about that," Cliff said. "In fact I wasn't even thinking about it. What I did think of and for the first time just a little while ago is that there may be something in the books that Clare herself might want destroyed if she knew it existed and that Fox Fur or whoever else came in is after."

"But I don't get it," Squeak wailed. "I don't understand what you're driving at."

"Blackmail." Cliff spoke the word in two distinct syllables. "Wake up, Squeak! Your own grandfather said there was something odd about her suddenly leaving the theater."

Before Squeak could answer, the young man who had taken their list came back. "We can let you have thirty-seven dollars and seventy-five cents for the bulk of your books," he said, and handed Cliff the list. "And nineteen dollars for the first editions."

"Thanks," Cliff said. "We'll let you know by mail if we want to take you up."

To Squeak the words were of no more significance than the humming of mosquitoes. "Cliff, listen," she began when they were out on the street. "Even if there is something there Clare doesn't want known we—we couldn't sell it."

Cliff dropped her arm. "Of course not," he said, and there was a chill reproof in his tone Squeak had never heard from him before. "I'm not suggesting we go in for blackmail. In fact I wasn't thinking in terms of money or profit at all. You're the one who suggested we skip selling the books, remember."

Squeak stopped short on the cold, windy sidewalk while little whirlpools of city dust beat around her. "Cliff, I'm a fool. I was thinking so hard about autographs that when you brought that up about Clare I just burst out with something without thinking what it meant."

Cliff stared into a dingy shopwindow without speaking and in that instant Squeak knew she had to make a decision. Either she could put him off with a quick, clever apology, or she could tell him how her mind had worked and try and make him understand. He turned toward her, his eyes bleak with misery, and in that instant Squeak's mind was made up. "Cliff, listen. It sounds crazy, but I've always been like that. I think hard about something and right away it grows so big and wonderful in my mind that when I switch to something else I don't make sense."

Still he said nothing and Squeak went on, no longer caring if he thought she was childish and a fool as long as he knew that she was telling the truth. "I've done it for ages, building things up in my mind. Careers. Situations. I had a story I told myself called 'The Idyll,' about a dream man, and not so long ago, either, and now I know that it was all hocus-pocus romancing. This time my mind was spinning out treasure from autographs. I didn't think about what I said. I hardly knew it, Cliff, until I realized I'd insulted you."

"It's all right now," Cliff said, and he spoke quietly and very slowly as he pulled her arm into his own. "And thank you for telling me."

18

Mrs. Frostgate's Letter It was quarter-past twelve when they reached Fifth Avenue, and they realized they had only just enough time to ride uptown and meet Dr. Lawrence for luncheon. "We'll ask Gramps about selling autographs," Squeak said after they had boarded a bus, "but we won't tell him anything else."

"Check," Cliff said, and grinned at her approvingly. "We'll leave the dramatics to Clare Clayton."

Dr. Lawrence was already waiting for them in the marble and red plush foyer of Dragonetti's restaurant. "I'm sorry I can't go with you to the auction," he said when they rejoined him after washing up, "but you won't be doing any selling today anyway. Farquarson will simply want to look at your list and then make arrangements for the future. I believe he has his auctions planned weeks and even months ahead."

Cliff's expression changed and he opened his mouth to speak, but just then a waiter led them to the table Dr. Lawrence had reserved and by the time they were seated he had apparently changed his mind about speaking and listened in silence while Squeak told her grandfather about their morning.

"Blatz offered us thirty-seven dollars and seventy-five cents for the bulk of the books," Cliff said when Squeak had finished. "And nineteen dollars for the first editions. Do you think we'd better accept their offer, sir?"

Dr. Lawrence glanced at the lists, which were grimy and shopworn from much handling. "I have a group of friends who collect modern firsts," he said, and nodded to a smart-looking couple on the other side of the room. "If you want to make me a copy of this I'd be glad to send it on to them. And now, Squeak, suppose you and I put our minds on food."

He passed her the menu and as she saw his cuffs, white and starchy above his immaculate old hands, she was suddenly conscious of how wrinkled and grubby both she and Cliff still were in spite of their scrubbing. Grandpa's fastidiousness was legendary and she struggled to think of some way to apologize to him without being mean or disloyal to Cliff. At that moment Cliff handed over his penciled list.

"It's rather messy, sir," he said. "I am too as a matter of fact, but you know what secondhand bookstores are like. And you can't make an omelet without breaking eggs."

Grandpa Lawrence chuckled and Squeak settled down to enjoying her shrimp cocktail, secure in the knowledge that Grandpa and Cliff not only liked but understood each other. She listened to them discussing bookstores and prices and now it came to her that Cliff's quick common sense was a much better passport to friendship than elaborate and artificial good manners.

"You two have done a good job," Dr. Lawrence said, and put the penciled list in his billfold. "And now tell me the news of Stapleton. Anyone heard from Sunny yet?"

"Mum and Dad had a telegram on Thursday and she sounds wonderful," Squeak said. "She and Charlie are coming home on their way through to camp tomorrow and I can hardly wait to see her."

They talked about Stapleton and the school. When Cliff began to ask Dr. Lawrence about autographs, Squeak's heart soared upward. Of course that was the answer to Cliff's treasure. Mrs. Frostgate knew how he needed money and perhaps she had thought of leaving it to him in this way so that it couldn't by syphoned off into the main part of her estate. "Don't you think we might find something valuable?" she said out loud. "Mrs. Frostgate corresponded with all sorts of people."

"Possible, but not probable," Grandpa said. "But if you find anything let me know and I'll inquire about reputable dealers. And now how would you like to have crêpes Suzette for dessert? It's rather a specialty here."

"Wonderful," Squeak said, and Cliff nodded enthusiastically and a few minutes later Dragonetti himself was mixing and stirring on a little movable spirit lamp in front of them.

By the time they had finished Squeak was so comfortably stuffed she wondered if she could move. She managed to stand up, but as she did so the book which she had had on her lap during luncheon fell to the floor. Burns Mantle's *Best Plays of 1944–45*. Grandpa reached for the book as Cliff picked it up, and thumbed through the contents. "A very uneven year, as I remember it, but your friend Clare Post, Mrs. Clayton, was excellent." He turned to the chapter on *Valiant* and glanced at the cast of characters before he handed the book back to Squeak. "Ralph Kent, her leading man, was quite good too."

"Do you remember anything more about why she left the stage?" Squeak asked, and Grandpa Lawrence shrugged as he led the way downstairs.

"Haven't really thought about it since Christmas dinner," he said, "but just now, when I saw the name of her director, Hartley Barringer, it seems to me she had a fight with him toward the end of the run and broke her contract about going on the road. But I imagine the real reason why she hasn't gone back and why she flashed out at Ed Singleton is because she's too old for ingénue parts."

Squeak felt as though a large red balloon had been pricked to rubbery nothingness in front of her. She had expected something romantic and bizarre, but what she had just heard might have happened to Mrs. Hilsen, who was always fighting with her different employers and was extremely touchy about her age.

She went on thinking about it until Grandpa Lawrence left them at Farquarson's Auction Galleries and Cliff piloted her into the last empty seats in a crowded, smoky room.

"Eighteen dollars?" the auctioneer intoned. "Eighteen-fifty. Do I hear nineteen for this fine six-volume set of Frank Stockton? Thank you sir, nineteen. Twenty. Do I hear twenty-one?"

The prices are a lot higher than they were at the bookstores, Squeak thought, and just then Cliff spoke directly into her ear. "Don't look now, but later on. All the way in the back. It's Fox Fur!"

"*No!*" Squeak was so surprised that she spoke out loud. The people nearest her turned and stared, so she looked down at her catalogue, and a moment later glanced more covertly over her shoulder. The tall man in the last row was certainly Fox Fur. The brush of silver-black hair was unmistakable as well as the hard, rather arrogantly handsome face. He lifted his pencil to bid and Squeak turned and whispered: "Cliff. He's bidding. If he buys anything we'll find out his name."

"Maybe," Cliff whispered back, but an instant later they learned that Squeak was wrong. The man, whatever he was called, was so well known at the gallery that giving his name was unnecessary. The auctioneer intoned his "Going, going, gone!" His assistant nodded at the man in the back row and scribbled down a notation on the pad in front of him.

Squeak made a face, but Cliff only shook his head and wrote on the bottom of his catalogue. "We'll find out afterwards. I wonder if he's seen us?"

"Don't know," Squeak mouthed, and now as she turned to look back she was seized with a restlessness that had nothing to do with the hard collapsible chairs or the stuffy air of the auction rooms. If the man had already seen them and recognized them what would he do? Duck and run, or come up to them boldly and ask for the books he had left behind? It was impossible to tell, and as her mind raced on to the immediate and unpredictable future she lost all interest in what was going on around her. For what seemed like hours the auction dragged on at the same pace. A little later, as two assistants carried a pile of red morocco quarto volumes onto the auctioneer's platform, the atmosphere suddenly changed. Several of the men nearest Squeak stood up and a thin hawklike woman in black beckoned to one of the assistants. "Could we see them, please," she said, and motioned toward the quarto volumes with her harlequin glasses.

The auctioneer nodded to his assistants. The men lifted up the books and carried each of the volumes in turn around the auction room. Squeak saw the lavish color plates and nudged Cliff, who nodded.

"I guess this is it," he whispered, and underlined the name *De Mannaco History of Costume* in his catalogue. "The big bomb of the afternoon. Jeepers, they're starting the bidding at a hundred dollars!"

Squeak gripped Cliff's sleeve and now she was as excited as he was. "Look. That little old man who looks as though he'd come in here to keep warm just bid a hundred and fifty, and, Cliff! Fox Fur's bidding!"

At three hundred dollars the bidding divided between Fox Fur and the woman with the harlequin glasses. "Three-fifty, thank you, madam. Three-sixty. Three-sixty against you. Three-seventy." There was no sound now except the auctioneer's voice and the slight creak of an assistant's shoes as he moved up and down in front of the room eying the audience for bids.

At four hundred and ten the auctioneer's hammer came down for the last time. "Sold at four hundred and ten dollars."

"Cliff! He got it. Fox Fur!" Squeak instinctively rose from her seat and almost immediately dropped down again as the sudden surge of people behind her pushed the chair hard against the back of her knees. "And look, he's leaving."

The tall, dark man spoke to one of the assistants and had already reached the door before Squeak was on her feet again. "This way!" Cliff urged her forward, but by the time they reached the aisle the way in front of them was solidly blocked by a dozen or more people who, now that the most important item of the day was sold, stampeded toward the exit.

"Quiet, please." The auctioneer rapped on the desk in front of him. "There are other items of great interest still to be sold. We now come to Lot No. 309, a fine collection of children's books of the late nineteenth century. What am I offered?"

The people who were leaving quieted somewhat, but the bottle-neck by the door was still crowded, and by the time Cliff and Squeak found themselves in a narrow hallway above a dark flight of stairs the man with the silver-fox hair was gone.

"Let's go after him. Let's follow him to the street!" Squeak fairly sputtered with excitement, but Cliff was perfectly calm.

"Not a chance," he said, and gripped her wrist as though she were Johnny's age. "We've got to ask the gallery owners about our list, and then run like heck for the train."

"Cliff, you're crazy," Squeak began, but he had already turned back and was showing one of the assistants in an outer room the list and asking if the Farquarson Galleries would be interested in selling their books.

The man glanced over the list and handed it back with a contemptuous smile. "I'm afraid not," he said. "Our consignors are universities, bookstores, and established collectors. Where'd you sweep this stuff up, in your grandma's attic?"

Squeak fully expected an explosion, but Cliff only ran his hand through his red hair and grinned disarmingly. "O.K.," he said. "And now I wonder if you could tell us the name of the tall dark gentleman who bought the *De Mannacos?*"

"He's Hartley Barringer, the producer. Owns one of the finest collections of books on the theater in the country. He's the man who directed *Jamboree* last winter."

"Thanks," Cliff said, and left the room with Squeak almost bursting with excitement behind him.

"Cliff, did you hear that's Hart——" She never finished her sentence, because Cliff's hard young hand pushed firmly against her mouth and stayed there while he motioned to her to look down the stair well. For an instant she only stared, and then as her eyes focused in the poor light she saw a man leave the telephone booth. As he hurried toward the door she recognized Fox Fur.

"It's him!" she burst out when Cliff finally took down his hand. "Cliff Hawks, whatever are we going to do now?"

"Catch the train," Cliff said, and added more grimly, "At least I hope so. We have exactly twelve minutes in which to reach Grand Central."

They made the train with a precious minute to spare and Squeak opened the Burns Mantle book even before she took off her hat or her coat. "Cliff, Fox Fur *was* her director. It says it right here. Hartley Barringer. And what do you bet he's the person who was in the shed both times and that he is looking for something connected with Clare?"

"Perhaps." Cliff was maddeningly calm. "But I don't see how he ever could have taken my key and put it back again."

"He could have arranged it." Squeak dismissed that detail. "And, Cliff, we'll go over every leaf and paper and clipping tonight and turn it over to Clare. The family are going out for dinner and I'm taking care of Johnny. I'll scramble us some eggs, and then we'll shake out every book in the place. Golly, I'm excited."

"So am I," Cliff said, and reached into his pocket for Mrs. Frostgate's letter. "Read this, Squeak, and then say you understood about last Sunday. I had a bad time before that man at Farquarson's turned us down, but if we've decided to sell to Blatz we're just about finished. I'd have died if there had been more weeks of waiting."

Squeak stared up at him and then looked down at the letter he held out to her and read to herself:

Dear Cliff:

You and I have always complimented one another by plain speaking and I am not going to insult you now by telling you that sharing my beloved books will turn you into a scholar or make you rich. I have no idea what profit half the proceeds of those you sell will bring you, but I count on you to do your best in driving a bargain. Your quickness and stubborn industry will make you a good businessman and therefore the perfect partner for my dreamy and unbusinesslike Serena. She has become a very pretty girl as well as a dear one, but she still has, and I hope will always keep, a sensitive and romantic attitude toward life and people which will make her vulnerable. Because of this I would not force upon her the close companionship of any young man unless it were someone like yourself, whom I trust as I trusted my only son. Your good common sense will guide you and I know I need not to be too specific, but perhaps it would be wise to say that no matter how you come to feel about Squeak you should not express your feelings until you have settled the matter of this joint inheritance.

I am old enough to know that the people we love do not always like one another. It is possible that you two children may not get along at all, but even so I am happy over my choice, not simply because I have little else I can leave you, but because I know each of you is strong enough in his and her own way to stay himself, and generous enough not to try to change the other. You won't read John Donne, dear Cliff, and I can't say that I blame you, but no man living understands better than you what Donne meant when he wrote, "God would not turn men from their calling but mend them in it."

God bless you, dear boy,
Your devoted old friend,
Dorothea Frostgate.

As Squeak handed back the letter her eyes filled with tears. "Oh, Cliff!" was all she could say, and now, as he reached toward her, unconscious of the people around them, neither of them drew away.

19

Evening Visitor Squeak stayed in a golden haze of wonder and happiness long after the conductor had taken their tickets and they had settled back in their seats. "Cliff, when did you begin, when did you first start——"

"To love you?" Cliff said, and the three words set her blood pounding. "Oh, ages ago, when I was a little brat and you were so small you looked like a cross between a mouse and a brownie."

"But—but I thought first it was Alice, and then the whole family."

"Perhaps you're right, at that," Cliff said, and his eyes had the old teasing glint in them. "When I was ten and Alice was twelve I thought she was terrific and I still think your family's pretty special. The trouble with you is you don't appreciate them."

"Cliff, I do!" Squeak protested, but as he held out Mrs. Frostgate's letter as though it were a peace offering, she grinned up at him and read it through for the second time. "My, this is like her," she said when she had finished, and Cliff nodded.

"Isn't it though? I can almost hear her chuckle when she signed her name, and see her reach out for an envelope and then get sidetracked by the telephone or shouting an order to Anna Dugan. She did put your letter in the envelope she had addressed to me, you know. That's how I happened to read yours."

Squeak's mind flew back to Christmas afternoon in the Holly House barn and Cliff's face red and angry-looking as he had answered Clare. "It was like you, too," she said, "to know the mix-up was due to Mrs. Frostgate and not say anything."

"I needn't have read it all," Cliff said. Suddenly he straightened up in his seat and ran his hand through his red hair. "Squeak. That afternoon. The man who sneaked out of the barn as I came in and drove off afterwards in the big black car. It could have been Barringer."

"It probably was!" Squeak said, and little prickles of excitement arched along her spine. "You come straight home from the station with me and we'll start going over the books in the shed even before we eat."

"I can't," Cliff said, and his voice hardened. "If I go straight home Miss Petersen will still be at Grandma's and this is the first chance I've had to see her since my key was moved. But I'll hurry down to your house as fast as I can after I've seen her. Maybe you could go through your books in the meantime."

A few weeks, even days ago Squeak would have argued. Now she knew that for some reason she couldn't entirely understand, the moving of the key was enormously important to Cliff and that for the time being, at least, he couldn't talk about it. "All right," she said quietly. "I'll be all ready to go up to the shed as soon as you can get down." He gave her hand a quick, grateful squeeze and a few moments later the train pulled into Stapleton.

Mr. and Mrs. Bruce and Johnny were all waiting for them on the station platform. "Did you have a good time?" Mrs. Bruce asked. "How was Grandpa?"

"Did you get a lot of money?" Johnny wanted to know. "And what did you have to eat?"

"I want to know too," Mr. Bruce said, and glanced at his watch.

"But you'll have to tell us in the car. The train's late and we have to get over to the Sturgises' in South Centreville in time for seven-o'clock dinner."

Squeak hurried along the cold, dark platform, past the winking oil lamps of the station house to the waiting car. Nothing had changed. Even the piles of snow at the edge of the parking lot were the way they had been that morning, and yet as far as she was concerned the whole world had erupted into a sparkling radiance of joy. She wondered if her own face showed the change, and slid into the back seat of the car, glad of its cavelike darkness. Then, as they drove off and the family went on peppering Cliff and herself with questions and giving out news of their own day, she knew no one had noticed.

They left Cliff at his grandmother's house and as he hurried up the short path Mrs. Bruce looked after him approvingly. "I must say I think he was very philosophical about the price Blatz offered you. I was so afraid he was going to be bitterly disappointed."

"We're going to have hot dogs for supper," Johnny said before Squeak could put in a word. "And I'm going to roast 'em in the fireplace. You like them that way, don't you?"

"Sounds wonderful!" Squeak said. A moment later Mr. Bruce slowed down to let them out by the path to the back door.

"Go to bed early, darling," Mrs. Bruce said. "You've had an exhausting day."

"Oh, I feel fine," Squeak said, and added quickly, "And Cliff's coming down to go over the books to see if they're any autographs or anything like that laid away in them that might be valuable."

Mrs. Bruce looked worried and for a moment Squeak was afraid that she had said too much. "Oh dear, I do hope Cliff isn't counting on finding a fortune tucked inside the books," Mrs. Bruce went on. "It's most unlikely."

"Oh, I know that and so does he," Squeak said, and gave an inward sigh of relief as Dad let in the clutch.

"Don't stay up too late," Mum called out, and Squeak waved to them in the darkness.

"We won't!" she called back, and now, as she hurried into the house, she was so anxious to get at the books themselves that the idea of dramatizing what had happened at the auction gallery never occurred to her.

Squeak went up to her own room and, taking off her city clothes, put on dungarees and a sport shirt. Since the week before Sunny's wedding she had really made an effort to keep her room tidy. Now as she looked around her, it occurred to her that for the first time her tidiness seemed worth the trouble. The very fact that she had kept the books which she had brought down from the shed together and neatly arranged them on a single shelf would speed up the job of going through each one.

As soon as she had finished dressing she pulled out *The Forsyte Saga* and, holding the cover in both hands, let the pages swing open above her bed. A receipted bill, a crossword puzzle clipped from a newspaper, a calendar for the year 1937. There was nothing more. She went through the books one by one. By the time she had finished her bed was littered with miscellaneous clippings, recipes, invitations, and pressed flowers, but there was nothing that could possibly be of value, nor, with the exception of a brief note from Clare Clayton thanking Mrs. Frostgate for some flowers, was there anything even remotely connected with Clare.

She had just piled the little collection together to show Cliff, when Johnny came in and spread it out again with one quick push. "Jeepers, what's all this stuff? Can I have the cutouts and the tin foil?" and in the next breath, "Come on down and eat. I'm practi-

cally starved and the hot dogs keep slipping off the toasting fork.
I've burned two, but you won't tell, will you, Squeak?"

"I won't tell," Squeak reassured him, and after she had gathered
up her findings again hurried downstairs. They had their supper
and while Squeak washed up Johnny went upstairs and put on his
pajamas and bathrobe without being told. He came down again
looking pink and white and angelic just as Cliff came in.

"Hi, Johnny. Squeak, let's go up to the shed," Cliff said, and it
was clear from his face and his quick, excited gestures that he had
something to tell her. "Let's move."

Squeak reached for her ski jacket, as eager to be off as Cliff, and
then Johnny stepped in front of the door. "I don't think it's fair,"
he said, and now he looked more like a small angry boxer than an
angel. "When somebody says they're going to sit with somebody I
think they ought to sit in the house and not way off in a cobbler's
shed!"

For an instant Squeak was stymied, but as she looked from
Johnny to the collection of odds and ends she had dropped on the
hall table, she was suddenly inspired. "Johnny," she said, and
thrust the little pile toward him. "You can have these for real keeps
if you'll take them up and look 'em over in bed right now!"

"Well, I don't know." Johnny had the long end of the bargain
and he apparently knew it. "What if I wanted something awful
bad while you were up at the shed? Then what could I do?"

"Ring the claxon bell. The one you got for Christmas." This time
Cliff had a brain wave. "We'll hear that easily and come running."

"Promise?"

"I promise," Squeak said, and a few minutes later Johnny was
settled down in bed with the odds and ends spread over his
coverlet.

"That was close!" Squeak said when she and Cliff were finally on their way up to the shed. "If Johnny'd really kicked up about our going to the shed we'd have been stuck."

"Teamwork," Cliff said, and Squeak could feel him grinning as she held the flashlight while he unlocked the padlock on the cobbler's shed. "But Squeak, listen, my key was used, all right. But Grandma didn't know a thing about it. She was asleep all last Sunday afternoon, Miss Petersen said. She didn't even know anyone had called."

Squeak looked over at Cliff as she straightened up from lighting the oil stove. Despite the cold he had pulled off his skiing cap and jacket, pushed the pencil at a rakish angle behind his ear, and was moving around the shed as though the space were too small to hold his exuberance. "But—who—but why—Cliff, I don't understand what you're talking about."

"I don't blame you," he said. "But the fact is as soon as I knew Mrs. Apsley was the only person who had called on Grandma that afternoon I thought she might have borrowed the key, but the thing that got me was that Grandma might have suggested it. Not to take anything, you know, but just to find out what I was doing or something like that. But Grandma didn't have anything to do with it. In fact she didn't even know that Mrs. Apsley had been in the house last Sunday."

"Are you sure Mrs. Apsley took the key? It couldn't have been someone else?"

"Not possibly. Miss Petersen let Mrs. Apsley in the first time and later in the afternoon when she sneaked in to put back the key Miss Petersen was in the kitchen, but she heard the door close and came out in time to see her car go off. I was a dope to think Grandma'd stoop to anything like that, but you know since she's been so lame she gets pretty desperate sometimes, wanting to know what goes on, and I guess I got to imagining things and feeling ashamed when there wasn't anything to be ashamed about. Boy, between that and not being able to explain last Sunday and not being sure how you felt, it's been one gruesome week!"

"But it's over!" Squeak said, and Cliff beamed at her.

"You bet!" he said. "And as long as Mrs. Apsley isn't any relation of mine I'm so happy I can be generous all over the place about the poor old fool snooping around just for the love of snooping. It's a cinch she's never even heard of Barringer and I doubt if she's done more than stare at Clare Clayton in church."

"But she has!" Squeak burst out, and for the second time that day her skin prickled with excitement. "I saw Mrs. Apsley talking to Barringer Christmas Eve and again up at the library, and I know she went to call on Clare Clayton last week and pumped her about everything!"

For an instant Cliff stood motionless. Then he wheeled toward the shelves and began frantically pulling out books. "So that's the answer!" he said as he held up one book after another by its board covers. "Whatever it is must be inside Clare's own books. They weren't here either time the shed was searched."

Squeak worked beside him and in twenty minutes they had gone through the whole collection of Clare's books but had found nothing. "She didn't stick things into books," Cliff said, and began at the left-hand end of the longest shelf of Mrs. Frostgate's collection. "And neither did Mr. Frostgate, so it must be among the old lady's books. You're sure that there wasn't anything important among that stuff you gave Johnny?"

"Positive," Squeak said. She stood still, trying to remember exactly what had been in the little pile of papers. She looked around her vaguely, and as she saw her father's workbench—covered with canvas and pushed into the furthest corner—her eyes darkened and an instant later she sprang forward. "Mrs. Frostgate's bedside books! You stuck them under the canvas the day Alice came up here!"

"Lord, yes!" Cliff burst out, and hauled back the canvas. They tore off the string that tied the books together and began to riffle through each volume separately. There were more flowers, notes, clippings, a yellowed wedding invitation, and a one-dollar bill. Then, from the pages of *St. Augustine,* fell a letter addressed to Mrs. Basil Clayton, Holly House, Stapleton, Conn., U.S.A.

Squeak reached out for it and as she saw the initials B.C. and the A.P.O. number in the left-hand corner she began to understand. "Cliff!" she said. "It's from Basil Clayton. Clare's husband. And Mrs. Frostgate never gave it to her."

"She plain forgot it, I guess. She was always doing things like that." He stared down at the letter as he spoke and now another thought struck him. "Squeak, when was he—Basil Clayton—killed?"

"In April 1945. Why?" Squeak said. When Cliff pointed out that the letter was dated 12 April 1945 she shivered. "Cliff, how—how pitiful. It was probably the last letter he ever wrote and Clare never got it. And—and Mrs. Frostgate would have been heartbroken if she'd known what she'd done."

"I know," Cliff said, and his voice was gruff with feeling. "I wonder if it makes sense to give it to her now. It might be ghastly for her."

"I'll give it to her," Squeak said, and for an instant, in spite of her perfectly genuine pity, she had a mental picture of herself dressed in the dinner gown she had seen in Wanamaker's, comforting a weeping Clare. The next instant Cliff's voice, once more intensely matter-of-fact and practical, brought her back to earth.

"Squeak, this letter hasn't a thing to do with what we're after. It's from Clare's husband, so it couldn't be blackmail or anything like it. If we want to help Clare we'll have to find out what

196

Barringer and perhaps Mrs. Apsley were after, and then give Clare this letter tomorrow after we've spoken to your family about it."

"I suppose so." Squeak reluctantly put down the letter on the workbench. "Maybe."

"Not maybe, positively!" Cliff said, and they set to work again.

They worked without speaking for perhaps five minutes, and then they both heard the sound of a car driving up over the frozen field toward the shed. "Why, how funny," Squeak said. "I didn't think the family would be home this early." The next instant the door of the shed opened and Hartley Barringer walked in!

"What are you doing here?" Cliff burst out. Squeak dropped the book in her hand and gaped, but Hartley Barringer looked completely at ease.

"Good evening," he said pleasantly. "It's good luck my catching you both here. I've just heard you're about to move out and I wanted to claim my books before you resold them. I suppose you still have them?"

"Yes." Cliff reached for the books, but Barringer took off a pair of expensive-looking chamois gloves before he accepted them. "Did you forget them?"

"Yes, stupid of me, wasn't it? And as you didn't know my name and address you couldn't forward them. I should have left word for you at Farquarson's this afternoon. I saw you both, but didn't get a chance to say hello. Still, as I was driving up this way for Sunday, I thought I'd stop in."

"We saw you too," Cliff said, but Squeak felt too deflated even to speak. Their mystery which had seemed to be growing only a few moments ago was suddenly blown into nothingness. Mrs. Apsley had probably gone through the books on both occasions and this well-dressed, prosperous-looking man had nothing more on his mind than picking up a couple of books he had more than paid for.

Mr. Barringer put down his hat, his gloves, and the books in a neat pile, and moved toward the workbench, rubbing his hands appreciatively. "Find any interesting covers?" he asked. "I should think this might be quite a likely place for a real find."

"We weren't looking for stamps!" Cliff said. As Barringer reached out in the direction of Clare Clayton's letter, Cliff snapped it up just ahead of him. "That letter isn't for you, Mr. Barringer."

The tall man coughed slightly. "It isn't for you either, is it? I thought I read that it was addressed to Mrs. Basil Clayton."

"That's right." For the first time since Barringer had come into the shed Squeak was able to speak. "We're going to give it to her tomorrow."

"I wouldn't do that," Barringer said. "Old wounds reopened can be more fatal than new ones and Clare's last months with her husband were not happy. As a matter of fact, ever since I learned that this letter might turn up among the old lady's things I've been hoping against hope Clare would never find it."

Cliff fingered the envelope uncertainly and Barringer pressed forward. "Better give it to me," he urged. "I'll take full responsibility for destroying it. After all, I'm Clare's oldest and most intimate friend."

"That isn't true," Squeak burst out. "Don't give him the letter, Cliff. Clare can't stand him."

Barringer looked pained. "We had a slight misunderstanding," he said, "but now that she is back in this country I'm sure it will soon be straightened out. Actresses are notoriously temperamental, but they are also very generous."

Cliff pushed the letter back in his pocket. "What Squeak says goes with me," he said firmly.

"Look here," Barringer rapped out, and it was clear he had lost patience. "You're both decent kids and I didn't want to have to tell

198

you this, but Basil Clayton was living with another woman while he was in England. I'm morally certain this letter is asking Clare for a divorce. Since she didn't know anything about it and Basil Clayton is dead it's sheer cruelty to let her read it now."

"He's lying!" Squeak's voice was shrill with anger. "Clare went to England just so she could talk to the people who had seen her husband last. She told me that herself."

Barringer shrugged. "What of it?" he said. "No decent human being would tear her heart by telling her the truth."

Squeak hesitated, suddenly miserable with uncertainty, and then Cliff rapped out, "I wouldn't bet on that! Mrs. Apsley would glory in telling anybody anything."

Barringer started. "You country people understand each other, don't you?" he said. "Mrs. Apsley told me earlier and again this afternoon over the phone that there was only one thing *you* were interested in, and that's money. All right, you win. I'll offer you one hundred dollars for that letter."

"So you can use it for blackmail?" Cliff said. "Not a chance."

Barringer put back his head and laughed and the sound was harsh and ugly. "Likely, isn't it? When my income's probably twenty times as large as Clare Clayton's ever was. She came back to this country because she was nearly broke, you know. Do be reasonable. You saw me at that auction today and you know I can afford what I want. I'll give you two hundred dollars cash and you can see me tear up the letter."

Squeak stared at Cliff's white face and for an instant her mouth was dry with fear. "Cliff, don't!" she whispered. The next moment they all heard the wild, incessant shrieking of Johnny's claxon-bell.

20

Squeak Knows the Score For an instant they stood staring stupidly at one another, and then as the clatter went on Barringer rapped out, "What in God's name is that?"

"Only Johnny. That's Squeak's kid brother," Cliff said casually, and pushed his hand up behind his ear. "He's all alone in the house and he probably wants a 'dink of water.'"

Barringer had opened the door and taken a few hurried steps outside, and now as he came back the papers which they had collected fluttered off the workbench. Cliff picked them up and pushed them at Squeak. "Better take these down before they blow away," he said, and his eyes, as they bored into hers, were darker than ever. "I'll keep Clare's letter so that Mr. Barringer and I can talk about it until you come back."

"Cliff, you won't. You can't . . ." Squeak began, but now Johnny's bell sounded louder than ever and Barringer gave her a push toward the door.

"Go to him, for heaven's sake!" he ordered. "Do you want to raise the whole countryside?"

She started to run toward the house, drawn as much by the raucous command of Johnny's bell as by the force of the man behind her. "Johnny!" she shouted. "Johnny! I'm coming."

Finally he heard her and drew back from the window. By the

time she rushed into the front door and dropped the handful of papers on the table he was halfway down the stairs. "Squeak!" he burst out, and she saw his face was red and tearstained. "The telephone woke me up and when I answered it there wasn't anyone there and I got lonely and scared and I thought you were never coming!"

He flung his small pajama-clad body against Squeak and for a moment she felt desperate with indecision. She couldn't leave Johnny alone now that he was actually shaking with fright, and yet she had to get back to the shed. She thought of telephoning the family, but she knew the Sturgises lived over twelve miles away and by the time they reached home it would be too late. "Johnny, I've got to get back to the shed," she said, and led him down the stairs. "But just for a few minutes, Johnny. And if you're good you can sit down here and watch for us out of the library window."

Johnny eyed her uncertainly. "No-o . . ." he began, and then as they passed the hall table he reached forward eagerly. "Did you find money?" he asked, and pointed to the dollar bill. "Is that why you have to go back?"

Squeak swept the papers, with the dollar bill on top, into his lap. "If you'll stay right here you can look over the other things and keep anything you want."

"Boy!" Johnny looked up with the last tears still trickling down his rosy cheek. "D'you promise? Will Cliff let me keep the dollar?"

"Yes! Yes, of course!" Squeak said, and then as Johnny picked up the bill she saw the two words that Cliff had somehow managed to scrawl across an old menu card. "Call Clare."

Squeak's heart soared as she raced for the telephone. It was the one possible solution and Cliff, whom she had suspected of falling for an offer of money, had thought of it! She reached for the receiver and at that moment there was a knock on the front door and Clare Clayton walked in.

"Clare!" Squeak dropped the receiver and ran toward her. "Oh, Clare. Thank God you've come!"

Clare looked from Squeak to Johnny in bewilderment. "What's happened? Is anyone hurt? I telephoned a few minutes ago and I couldn't get an ans——"

Squeak pushed her toward the door, calling back over her shoulder, "Johnny, you stay there. Clare and Cliff and I'll be back in no time!"

"I don't understand," Clare began, as Squeak slammed the door. "Johnny looks terribly upset and do you really think we ought to leave——"

"Barringer!" Squeak burst out. "Up in the shed. Now. Trying to buy a letter of yours. From your husband!"

"Squeak, are you mad?"

"No." Squeak struggled for calmness as though it were a rope just out of her drowning grasp. "No, Clare, listen. It was a letter he wrote to you from England. Mrs. Frostgate put it in one of her books and forgot it. Cliff has it now and Barringer's trying to buy it from him."

For a fraction of a second Clare stood still. Then pulling her wrap more closely around her, ran swiftly toward the shed.

She was at the little rise before Squeak caught up with her. "Cliff—won't—sell!" Squeak panted, but Clare had already opened the door and run inside.

Barringer, who had been facing Cliff with his back to the door, wheeled. "Clare! How did you get here?"

Clare did not even look at him. For an instant there was no sound except her own and Squeak's quick breathing, and the crackle of paper as Cliff pulled the letter out of his pocket and

202

handed it to her. "I'm glad you came," he said. "Your friend Mr. Fox Fur Barringer won't believe he can't buy anything he wants."

"Clare. Please! Listen!" Barringer broke in. "This is too fantastic, but it's all because of these darned kids. Will you please put down that letter and let me explain?"

Still Clare said nothing and her face, as she looked from the letter to Barringer, was without expression. "It is from Basil," Barringer said. "And I learned from Mark Rollins just before Christmas that it had been sent here and that by some absolutely providential fluke you never received it."

"And you don't want me to read it now?" Clare's voice was polite and withdrawn and Barringer leaned forward to press home his advantage.

"No. No. I don't for your own good, Clare. I admit I did get Basil into that U.S.O. tour. I freely admit that, and that I asked him not to tell you I'd had anything to do with it until he came home. But that was for your sake, Clare. You must understand that. If he had played opposite you in *Valiant* it would have been a Basil Clayton not a Clare Post show and——"

"I have realized that since Basil's death," Clare said, and although her eyes never left the letter Barringer moved back as though she had struck him.

"So that's why . . ." he began, and then with a visible effort launched into another attack. "But you must not read the letter now, Clare. It will only distress you. Bring you back to the past and what you must do is face the present and——"

Clare's head lifted and, as she moved toward Barringer, Squeak had the illusion that she grew inches with every step. "If you leave now and promise that I will never see you again this whole episode will stop here," she said. "But if you don't go—at once—I will ask Cliff to call the police."

Cliff, who was nearest the door, reached for the doorknob and Squeak saw he was grinning like a gargoyle. "Squeak will go," he said. "I'm staying in case he gets rough."

Barringer laughed, but the sound fell flat. "Melodramatic company you're keeping, Mrs. Clayton. In fact distinctly ham." No one spoke, and then, as Cliff pushed Barringer's hat, gloves, and books toward him, he shrugged. "Still, you're plenty old enough to know your own mind."

"We are waiting for you to leave," Clare said coldly. A moment later Barringer slammed the door behind him and they heard the engine of his car.

"A really nasty customer," Cliff said, and picked up his pencil from the floor and pushed it behind his ear. "And he simply can't believe that the whole world isn't an auction where he'll always have the highest bid."

"I know," Squeak said, and then she saw that Clare Clayton had opened her letter. She stood still for a second, torn with curiosity and an almost irresistible impulse to make the most of what was going to be real drama. She swallowed fast and, gripping Cliff's sleeve, pulled him toward the door. "Johnny's waiting," she said. "Clare will come down to the house as soon as she's finished."

They walked beyond the light of the cobbler's shed. Then Cliff stopped short and pulled Squeak close. "You're a wonder," he said, and kissed her. "An absolute knockout. You understand how Clare feels and you knew just how I felt about that money."

"I know it was ghastly," Squeak said, and now she drew away from him, made shy by the memory of her own distrust. "And I wasn't sure, not absolutely sure, what you were going to do, because you'd said maybe Clare oughtn't to see that letter, and then I found your scribble. Cliff, when did you manage that?"

"When Fox Fur ran out to find out about Johnny's bell. I'd just dropped the pencil as he came back and I was scared stiff he'd notice."

"But he didn't," Squeak said. "Oh, Cliff, you were terrific."

"It wasn't hard once I knew he was lying," Cliff said, and burst out laughing. "You know, I've just thought that perhaps he was offering me stage money."

"Cliff, no!" Squeak stopped short as they reached the front door. "You're kidding."

Cliff shrugged as they went inside. "We'll never be able to prove it," he said. "But if he didn't think of it I don't see why he didn't. If we'd sold him a letter that didn't belong to us we couldn't have made a peep."

Squeak stared at him, and suddenly laughed so that Johnny came flying out into the hall. "Say, are you two nuts?" he demanded. "And where's Mrs. Clayton? And Squeak, did you ask Cliff if I can have the dollar?"

"No, but you can," Cliff said, and as he rubbed the dollar as though to prove that that at least was real, Squeak burst out laughing all over again. Just at that moment Clare came into the hall and as Squeak looked at her white, controlled face the laughter dried in her throat. Cliff looked at his shoes and Johnny ran toward Clare. "Did you telephone this house? The ring woke me up, but when I answered there was only buzzing."

"Yes, I did." Clare kissed the top of his head before she turned to Cliff and Squeak. "I didn't know Barringer was here," she said. "I came because Mrs. Apsley stopped in to see me about an hour ago in an absolutely hysterical state, protesting that she hadn't meant any harm to you and that she didn't pretend to understand theatrical people or their friendships. Do you suppose Barringer had been working on her to get that letter?"

"I'm sure of it!" Cliff said. "Squeak's seen them together several times starting way back with Christmas Eve. He was up here then, wasn't he?"

"Yes," Clare said. "He'd heard about the books and told me he thought there might be something he might want. He simply wouldn't believe me when I said they were yours. In fact I'm morally certain he went to look at them in the Holly House barn Christmas afternoon. That was one reason why I was so relieved when you decided to move them down here."

"Cliff guessed that!" Squeak said, and Cliff went on, "The sixty-four-dollar question now is Mrs. Apsley's connection with Barringer. What do you bet that until he telephoned this evening and told her he was coming up here she really believed he was a good friend of yours? He gave us a line about its being kinder not to show that letter to you and if I hadn't caught on that Mrs. Apsley was involved I might have thought he was sincere."

"It all fits in," Clare said slowly. "She kept telling me I was putting temptation in your path and that I must go over those books myself tonight. Then when I said I was going to telephone your father she said something about thanking God if it wasn't too late and literally fled out of the house. As you know I tried to telephone and when I couldn't get an answer I was really worried, so I drove right down."

"Thank goodness!" Squeak said, and Johnny yawned noisily and grinned up at Clare Clayton.

"I'm glad too," he said. "I don't like going to bed with just kids in the house. It's much cozier when there is somebody old like you around."

Squeak's mouth opened, but long before any words came Clare had reached down and given Johnny a hug. "I don't blame you," she said. "And now if you'll take me up to your room I'll tuck you in and that'll be really cozy."

"Sure!" Johnny scrambled up the stairs and as Clare started to follow him she turned and handed Cliff the letter. "I wish you two would read this," she said. "It'll explain a lot of things you need to know."

Cliff took the letter, and as Clare disappeared he walked into the library and without saying a word held it out so that both he and Squeak could read it.

"Darling love,

As usual these days I am writing to you from a very queer place. The public shelter in the Underground this time and old Mark Rollins is sitting opposite getting very pally with an ancient cockney with a sprig of nodding flowers in her hat and a fine, beery voice. If I were producing this show there'd be the sound of a hurdy-gurdy in the distance instead of bombing and you, my darling, would come on centre stage and recite Alfred Noyes' *The Barrel-Organ*. Oh, Clare, I can hear your voice, the most beautiful in all the world, and the wonderful part of it is that I've come to understand and respect the people around me so well that I know every single one of the assorted characters in this shelter would revel in your voice as I do.

Such mixed up things come out of war. Death and dirt and pain and courage and for me, very recently, the most amazing kind of self knowledge. I know, once and for all, what I want out of life. You first, my darling, though that is not new, and our life in the theatre together and it is there in our profession that I've really made discoveries.

Last fall when Hartley Barringer put me on to this U.S.O. job I accepted with alacrity but I had my tongue in my cheek about his motives. I knew he wanted to feel that he had created you by giving you, as he has done, a play which would really challenge your ability and which would bring you a permanent niche in stage history. I also knew that he understood you well enough to know that if you realised he had wangled me into this overseas job you would never consent to work for him so I was perfectly happy to keep quiet about it. Now, though, I realise that the only thing that matters is that we have each played our parts up to the hilt and are ready to go on from there. An actor's job is to interpret man to himself and in order to do that he has to respect his fellow men enough to give them humour instead of slapstick, character instead of mannerisms, and glory instead of tinsel. If this means that after the war we'll be playing third rate towns in a company of our own, or even doing big parts here in London, I know you, my darling love, will go along with me.

I'm going to give this letter to Mark to mail to you at Holly House because I go to sleep at night thinking of you up there walking past those crazy stone lions into the orchard in that blue dress you wore when we went up to tell your cousin Dorothea we were engaged. Give the old lady my love, by the way. Does she still keep house with one hundred and one assorted birds and still lose her glasses and everything else but the kitchen stove in the book she is reading?

There's hope in the air, Clare love, and I think pretty soon I'll be able to write that I am coming home.

With all my heart,
Basil.

Squeak could not see for the tears as Cliff silently folded the letter, and they were both startled as Clare came back into the room. "Johnny's in bed," she said, and took the letter from Cliff, "and you have both read this?"

Squeak nodded, not trusting herself to speak, and Clare went on in the same quiet, perfectly controlled voice. "Would your family mind if I put in a long-distance call to Mark Rollins?" she asked. "I think he'll be able to tell us the things we still don't understand."

"Of course they wouldn't mind!" Squeak jumped to find the telephone book, glad to be doing something—anything—for Clare Clayton.

Clare smiled and as she reached for the receiver Cliff beckoned to Squeak. "We'll go lock up the shed," he said, and when she had followed him outside into the frosty moonlight he took her arm. "I don't care a hoot about locking it and I know you don't. It's just a way of giving Clare a break. She—she's wonderful, Squeak. You were right all the time and I got fooled by the window-dressing."

For several moments as they walked over the crunchy ground Squeak said nothing. "I've been fooled thousands of times," she said. "About you, about my own family, about myself. Even tonight I started to spin out a lot of rubbishy nonsense in my mind, but I woke up in time."

Cliff turned off the stove and the light and carefully locked the door. "Mistakes are too bad," he said as they started back toward the house. "But the big thing is to be able to admit them, and that's what I've learned from you, Squeak."

She looked up at him, yearning to hear more, but he shook his head. "Not now," he said gently. "I can see Clare's finished telephoning."

They walked into the front hall and Clare came out to meet them. "I reached Mark," she said, "and he knew all about that letter, but he never realized until last fall, shortly after I came home and we talked about Basil, that I had never received it. Mark couldn't bear to tell me about it. Later on, just before Christmas, he saw Hartley Barringer. When Barringer boasted he could get me to play bit parts for him any time he wanted me, Mark told him that letter had been written and might, conceivably, still turn up. Mark felt, you see, that if Barringer knew about that letter he'd never dare bother me again."

"Was that why Mr. Rollins looked so angry Christmas Eve?" Squeak asked.

"In a way. You see, Mark had come up to offer me a small character part and I wouldn't even discuss it. In fact I made him take me to church so that he couldn't talk about the theater at all. Then when he saw that Barringer was up here he jumped to the conclusion that I'd signed up to do a Barringer play. Of course eventually I convinced Mark that I hadn't, but in the meantime Barringer had seen enough of this community and heard enough about Cousin Dorothea to believe that the letter might turn up and that all he had to do was intercept it, and sooner or later I'd let him direct me in anything he liked. Barringer could never understand, you see, that at the time of Basil's death I already knew that if I hadn't played in *Valiant* Basil wouldn't have gone overseas. It was a sense of guilt that drove me out of the theater. Guilt and grief. But now, after what I've learned from Basil's letter and from you two and Johnny, I'll go back."

"From us?" Cliff's face wrinkled with surprise and Squeak added, "From us and Johnny?"

Clare smiled, and suddenly acting, she stooped and reached forward with an imaginary cane. "I'll be playing old, old women," she croaked, and laughed at their faces. "I've known for a long time, you see, that Basil would never have wanted me to leave the stage. But the part that Mark offered me was that of a mother, a commonplace woman of my own age, and not the lead. Even a month ago I didn't have the courage or the wisdom or the plain horse sense to be willing to face facts and the calendar."

At that moment they heard the sound of the Bruces' car and Clare stood up facing Cliff and Squeak. "Will one of you tell Mr. and Mrs. Bruce what's happened?" she said. "They must know, of course, but I don't want to upset and alarm them unnecessarily."

"Squeak will tell them," Cliff said, and it seemed to Squeak that she never had a handsomer compliment. "She knows the score."

21

Love Learns by Laughing   The next morning when Squeak went downstairs her father had already gone off to take Clare Clayton to see Mrs. Apsley, Johnny was at Sunday school, and mother had breakfast ready for her on a tray. "You'd better hurry, darling," she said. "We're to meet Dad and Clare at church and all come back here for lunch together."

For once Squeak needed no urging and a few minutes later they drove off. As they turned onto the road Squeak looked back at the shed, which looked so small and ordinary in the daylight that it was hard to believe so much had happened there only the night before. "Golly, Clare was wonderful," she said, and her mother nodded.

"And so were you and so was Cliff," she said. "I'm proud of all three of you."

Squeak said nothing, but suddenly the fact that she and Clare and Cliff were grouped together in Mum's mind was the nicest part of the compliment. "Walk proudly friended." Words that were underlined in Mrs. Frostgate's scrapbook came to her and she smiled to herself as Mum drove up to the shed behind the church where Dad and Clare Clayton were waiting for them.

"Mrs. Apsley ate out of our hands," Dad said. "She's practically prostrate with apologies."

Clare nodded. "Cliff Hawks was absolutely right," she said. "Barringer apparently picked her out as a natural ally the first time he came up here. He could see she was a busybody and gossip with endless prejudices against actresses and the younger generation. He told her the same lies about Basil he told you and led her on to thinking that Cliff would hold onto that letter for money if Barringer didn't get it first. She didn't have any idea of what she was really doing!"

"But she's learned now!" Dad said. "And I think from now on she'll mind her own business."

Mum laughed. "Then you've done the community a great service," she said. At that moment they saw Johnny come out of the Sunday-school room and hurry down the slope toward them.

"I'm going to stay for church," he called when he was halfway down the hill, "'cause they're playing 'Onward Christian Soldiers' and I hope it'll be a short sermon."

Squeak giggled and he turned and ran back to the church. "I guess we had better go too," Mum said, and she and Clare started to walk toward the church together.

Mr. Bruce looked down at Squeak inquiringly, but she shook her head. "I'm going to wait to tell Cliff what you and Clare just found out," she said. "Cliff's never late."

They walked around to the front of the church and there, as though in proof of Squeak's words, they both saw Cliff, his red hair glistening in the sunshine, hurrying down the village street toward them. Mr. Bruce went on in and Squeak told Cliff what she had just heard. He listened silently, and as she finished his sharp, alert face suddenly brightened with a lightning smile. "The funny part is that Mrs. Apsley really helped us in the end," he said as he reached for the handle of the church door. "How Mrs. Frostgate would have laughed over that!"

Squeak nodded and they went into the church and joined the family and Clare. Darling, wise, gay Mrs. Frostgate. How much had she guessed of all the things that had come out of her gift? It was only after the processional was over and Squeak heard Clare's voice beside her that she forgot Mrs. Frostgate and thought about Christmas Eve, which seemed years, not days, ago. She listened intently to the voices close to her. Mum's and Dad's, Johnny's, Cliff's, Clare's. Each voice so different and each in its own way so dear. She heard other voices too, behind her and in front, muttered and clear, old and young, male and female. "God emploies many translators." She remembered the words she had read in Alice's book before the carol service and her heart pounded with the joy of sudden understanding. "God emploies many translators." The voices around her, the people old and young, rich and poor, homely and beautiful—those voices—were all God's translators.

Cliff leaned toward her holding out the hymn book. She smiled at him and as the choir broke into the opening bars threw back her head and sang, " 'Glorious things of thee are spoken, Sion city of our God.' "

An hour later they were all back home and Sunday lunch with the four Bruces and Cliff and Clare seemed to Squeak as festive as the party the night before Sunny's wedding. The happiness, the lovely carefree feeling, lasted long after Clare had gone home and she and Cliff had changed into old clothes and gone to work loading the books into Clare's car. It was catching too, Squeak realized, as she watched Cliff pile parcel after parcel of books into the car and sing as he worked. " 'Oh, you can't go to heaven in powder and paint,' " Cliff sang.

" 'Oh you can't go to heaven in powder and paint.' " Squeak joined in as she reached for a pile of books. " 'Cause the Lord won't love you as you ain't. I ain't goin' to grieve my Lord no mo!'"

They had nearly finished loading the car when they heard the sound of Johnny's claxon-bell louder and noisier than ever as he ran toward them swinging the bell handle as he ran. "Sunny's home. Sunny's home! Come on down to the house!"

They rushed down to the house after him and they were still in the middle of greetings and hugs and exclamations when the telephone rang. Johnny answered it and then shouted, "Telephone for Cliff. Long distance!"

Mr. Bruce, still with his arm around Sunny, nodded toward the kitchen. "Better take it in there, Cliff, or you won't be able to hear yourself think."

Cliff disappeared and for a moment Squeak had eyes for no one but Sunny, who was back in her own old place on the window seat with Johnny curled up as close beside her as he could get. "Johnny says you've nearly finished the books," Sunny said, "and I think that's absolutely incredible. I don't see how they managed, do you, Charlie?"

"Sounds as though they'd worked overtime," Charlie said. He sat down beside Sunny and Squeak slipped off into the kitchen to find Cliff. He had finished telephoning and stood staring out of the window.

"Cliff, is everything all right? Who was that?"

"Your grandfather, Dr. Lawrence——" Cliff began, when Squeak interrupted. "The first editions! His friends want to buy them for thousands of dollars."

"They don't want to buy them at all." Squeak's face fell and Cliff moved quickly toward her, his arms outstretched. "But, Squeak, the terrific thing is that now the money doesn't matter. I've just realized for the first time, and maybe that's what Mrs. Frostgate

214

meant me to find out, that I can earn money on my own right here in Stapleton. Shoveling snow, furnaces, all kinds of odd jobs. If you're for me, Squeak, I can do anything!"

"Cliff. Cliff!" Squeak was in his arms and she stayed there until Charles Reed came out to the kitchen.

"Sorry!" he said, and as he started backing out he looked stiffer and starchier and more correctly military than ever. "I just told your mother I'd give you a hand with the tea tray."

"You do that!" Squeak said. "And Cliff and I'll bring in the crumpets and cake."

It was over an hour later when Cliff and Squeak finally went back to the shed for the last of the packing. Cliff switched on the bright overhead light and they both laughed as they looked at each other's dusty, grimy faces. "Boy, I'm filthy," Cliff said, and tried to rub the book dust off his hands. "How can you stand having me around after seeing Charlie Reed?"

"I'm not Sunny," Squeak said happily, and then another thought struck her. "Cliff, Cliff Hawks. When did you first start to love me?"

"I told you," Cliff said, and his voice was teasing. "Ever since you were about five years old."

"I don't mean that and you know it," Squeak said hotly, and Cliff's expression changed.

"I think it was really the day we started working up here," he said. "When you tried bluffing Tom Connaught and didn't get away with it. And then the day you told me that thing about warriors for the working day! Say it again, Squeak."

Squeak said the words slowly and clearly and at the last line Cliff joined in and they spoke together, " 'But, by the mass, our hearts are in the trim'!"

"That's us," Cliff said. A little later as he put the last of the books in the car and tucked the old canvas from the workbench over them he began singing, " 'Love learns by laughing first to speak, then slyly gains cares passing great.' "

"That's us too," Squeak said. "That's really us!"